LIVINGSTON

TRENTON SECURITY BOOK 1

J.M. DABNEY

HOSTILE WHISPERS PRESS, LLC

REMEMBER

PLEASE BE ADVISED

AUTHOR'S NOTE

This story contains scenes of extreme depictions of childhood trauma/violence. While it's not written in great detail some readers may find the content objectionable.

DEDICATION

To my readers who embrace my characters who come in all shapes, sizes, and shades. Who also believe that even the broken can be beautiful. A very heartfelt thank you to The Asylum Residents, you all know who you are. Special thanks to all the ones who kick my ass or remind me why I write. Tracey, Meredith, Michelle, Qhuinn, Claudia and Dan, I appreciate you all more than any of you will ever know.

PROLOGUE

ranger, Wyoming 1996
"Livingston, we've done all that we can. More surgery would just—"

Francis Livingston tuned out the doctor's voice. The same conversation on fucking repeat and it always ended the same way. He was stuck with the scars that covered seventy-five percent of his body. He fisted his hands on his thighs and tried not to take a swing at the older man. It wasn't the guy's fault. His mind wandered as it always did when he didn't want to hear the bullshit and it never went anywhere good.

"Go to bed, Francis, I'll be up to tuck you in," his mother ordered, her hands in the soapy water.

He'd thought it strange at the time. His mother never tucked him in—she barely acknowledged he existed. He remembered he'd walked through the living room. His siblings and the sister-wives were there, and they didn't pay attention to him either. Mr. Teller was indisposed with one of the other sister-wives. This one was due to be cursed with another child, but she was the oldest, and she hadn't given Mr. Teller a child in almost two years. He was born before the man his mother married had that fucked up ceremony. That bastard and his harem of plain, broken women, even at eight, he'd recognized it. Mr. Teller was quick to use his fists and belt to keep order in his house. He swung that leather punctuated with *The Word* and cowed the brainwashed occupants of the man's home.

He'd earned his mother's revenge. For every beating she received, he'd gotten the same, but only more severe. He could still clearly see the crazed look in her eyes and the way her hair came undone from her bun in her fury. Wasn't that what mothers did? He was evil, and he deserved his punishment. Love came in shades of blue and black, fading to a deceptively pretty purple and a sick greenish-yellow like the infection from his wounds in the early days of his treatment. All she required was him to repent, but for what? What had he done but be born?

When he'd reached his room, he'd changed into his pajamas, simple plaid and crawled into bed. He'd studied the cracks in the ceiling, discerned shapes from the flowing lines then again where they broke at another small fissure. He shared his room with his mother. Two iron beds, nightstands with their ever-present bibles. The unfinished floors with their cracked planks cut into his knees where they bowed as he read to his mother from that book. He never recalled a time he believed in those words—God so loving and kind, but that book told of horrors and people dying for so-called sins. Pretending became second nature, but he no longer feigned faith and never would.

His mother walked into his room that night with a smile, and that should've warned him of the hell to come.

"Francis, have you repented for your sins today?"

"Yes, mother."

"I believe you are lying to me and you know what happens to sinners."

Her voice so calm and serene, almost happy and apprehension had pooled in the pit of his empty stomach. They had deemed him ungrateful for the scraps they provided him and ordered him to sit at the table to watch the worthy eat. He remained silent. He didn't beg or move as she secured each ankle and wrist to the bed with the softness of scarves. He could take the pain—he'd survived it his entire life. His mother's first kind act could've been not letting him being born at all, but her selfishness won out. He knew she'd hoped to trap a man she thought was wealthy—who'd take care of her. When she'd left that city, she hadn't anticipated the other wives and children waiting or the house which practically crumbled around them.

She ranted as she beat him. Placed blame and he could repeat every word from memory—even eight years later.

He'd braced for the first strike, fist or leather—it hadn't mattered—it was just his life. It was his fault Mr. Teller wouldn't sleep with her anymore. No matter how many times Mr. Teller tried, Livingston's mother couldn't carry another baby.

He hadn't started begging not even when she turned off the light and disappeared. Minutes or hours could've passed, but by the time she returned the house had grown quiet. The click of the light beside her bed drew his attention, and he'd watched her, the laziness of her movements and still with that happy expression on her face. The scent of gasoline thick in the room, the odor burning his nose.

"Do you know why I'm doing this, Francis?"

She'd never called him anything other than his name, no son or cute nickname.

"I was bad."

It was the last words he spoke before a rag was shoved deep into his mouth, choking him as he tried to breathe. His clothes became soaked as his mother poured the contents of the small red container over him and the bed. After the sulfur and gas stench, everything went fuzzy, and he was all screaming agony as his sheets and clothes ignited. Before he'd passed out, all that was left was that peaceful smile.

He didn't know how he escaped with only one side completely burned, but it was enough. He had Mr. Teller to thank for his life and his misery. He touched the thick, straight scars hidden within the grotesque landscape of his wrist. The one he'd slit a year ago hoping it would end and it hadn't, and here he was being told that there was no more to be done.

"The scars will fade over the years, but trying another procedure will only intensify them. I'm truly sorry, Livingston, you're alive, you can live—"

"I can what, live a normal life, no one fucking looks at me, doc, and when they do they know, know what happened. Will I find someone someday who wants to suck the freak's cock, all the scarred inches of it? Will they whisper they love me? Will I ever walk down the fucking street and not—"

"Livingston, you survived a horrific act that would've killed most, why don't you accept God's—"

"Fuck God, was this part of your God's plan?"

"This was the act of a sick woman, not—"

"Save it, doc."

He didn't wait for more pretty, consolatory words that were nothing more than empty promises of a future he didn't have. He rushed outside and pulled out the crushed pack of smokes, and then he lit one as he let his gaze shift left and right along the nearly empty Main Street. This town loved their secrets and their God, two more years and he could leave this place.

He turned his back to the street as the big, battered Sheriff's vehicle cruised down the road. That fucker knew what was going on out at that farmhouse and always looked the other way.

"Shouldn't you be in school, Livingston?"

He spun on his toes, the brim of his cap low over his eyes and studied the brown chaw-stained lips.

"Doc appointment, I got a note and everything."

"Don't be a smartass, Livingston, you're going to end your ugly ass up in my jail one of these days, and I'm going throw away the fucking key."

"Try your best, old man."

He turned to head back toward his foster home and the razor that was waiting for him—for the time he wouldn't fail. By his own hands or the day he turned eighteen, he'd leave this fucking town, but his past was mapped in ridges of hollows of twisted skin. That was one thing he could never leave behind.

LINUS HAD TO BE FUCKING KIDDING HIM

*B*eing the beast without the escape clause worked in his favor—most of the time. Other times it added to the ugliness on his body. Twisted the grotesque landscape of his flesh even more. Liv removed his tactical vest, thigh holster, and shoved them into his locker. Trenton Security became his second home the minute his boss, Linus Trenton, had hired him on about seven years ago, but they'd known each other over a decade. He loved his job, more dangerous the better. Linus only gave him solo missions others would consider suicidal.

It was the only thing he lived for, and his boss knew it.

A loud rapping of knuckles on the door caused him to glance over his shoulder. His teammate Harmon Little filled the doorway with his customary mischievous grin on his face. The man was an overgrown kid.

"Liv, boss wants you in his office. He's got another death wish mission for you." Little hollered but didn't come into the room.

He smirked and slammed his locker door. He raised his hands and scrubbed them over his face, his fingertips and palm caught on the irregular planes of the scars. He'd memorized the dips and bumps on his ruined skin over the years.

He still remembered the fire licking at his body. The stench of burning hair and flesh, still as strong in his memory as when he was eight. Twenty years and sometimes the dreams were so vivid as if it'd just happened. He shook it off and went to find out his next assignment.

He strode quickly through the building, down hallways, then up to the third floor where their offices and conference rooms were. He entered through the open door without knocking. Linus was behind his desk with his phone pressed to his ear.

"Yeah, Yeah, I love y'all too. Yes, I wore my vest, Hunter, and no, Wren, everything went fine. Unless we're in bed stay off my balls, baby."

He snorted and took a seat to wait for Linus to finish with the call to his husbands. He had no idea how Linus handled two men; he could barely get one to look at him. But his boss seemed happy. Even took fewer risks than Linus normally did. They used to be the first to jump at the insane missions. He tuned out the conversation because he didn't want to listen to the lovey bullshit.

Finally, the call ended, and Linus turned toward him.

"Still digging the married life?"

"It has its moments."

"Little said you had an assignment for me."

He didn't want to rush the boss, but he was ready to go home and take a shower. Three-day stakeouts didn't exactly make for pleasant smells. And he wasn't one to get naked in the locker room. He was plenty used to what he looked like, but he wasn't up for looks of pity or no looks at all.

"Suspected stalker case. Simple bodyguard duty."

"Are you fucking kidding me? No fucking way."

"You saying no to an assignment?" Linus' voice was lethally quiet.

He knew that tone. Heard it plenty over their friendship but he hadn't heard it aimed his way before.

"You know I don't handle babysitting cases. You always send

Pure." Pure Warner was ruthless as all of them combined; they assumed it was to make up for the pretty face. The man was huge, but he had these boyishly innocent features. Pure was perfect for babysitting jobs. He had an innate ability for putting even the most traumatized at ease.

Now, him, not so much. His right side from his face to his toes was a patchwork quilt of burn and graft scars. The scars on his face were not as bad, but most of them were hidden by his beard. He'd found himself thankful for his ability to grow a beard when he couldn't really grow hair on the right side of his body. The damage had destroyed most of his hair follicles. He silently cursed himself for dwelling on the shit he couldn't change. His ugliest wounds were luckily under his clothes.

They'd put expanders under the skin on his back to cover the worst of his injuries.

"Pure has another assignment to handle. Little is a loose cannon. Gage has a full-time job keeping our asses out of trouble and or jail."

"Who's the client?"

"Fielding Haskell. He's an up and coming actor. About to make it big or at least that's what his agent says. Filming starts in four months, and they want him hidden away until it does."

"Four fucking months?"

Liv wasn't hearing this shit. He was not babysitting some fucking diva for months.

"Once we get him stashed out at your place, your security system rivals the fucking Pentagon...you can come to the office. Bring him with you. He lands in four hours out at Cam's place, since he's got the private airstrip for his men, we can sneak Haskell in."

Their friends Sin and Saint were married to the local Sheriff. They flew the rescue choppers for the Sheriff's department. Sometimes they even flew the Trenton team. They didn't do it often since Sheriff Camden Pelter was obsessively protective of his boys.

"I gotta go home and shower off three days' worth of stench. How Little crashes in his van fucking astonishes me."

"You ain't fighting me on this, Liv?"

"Would it do any good?"

"Not at all. Meet out at Cam's place at 0100 hours."

"Got it."

He didn't wait around, just grabbed the file Linus handed him and hurried to his SUV. Bulletproof from top to bottom, even with the tires taking a hit, they'd get him several more miles. Some called him paranoid, but he was simply cautious.

He pulled out his fob, hit the remote starter and hopped into the driver's seat. It was forty-five minutes out to his cabin and then almost an hour to Cam's place. So he didn't have much time to get home, get showered and prepare his place for a guest. Hope the guy didn't require a lot of privacy. One room, one bed, he'd set up a bedroll, and be nice and give the kid the bed. He had slept in worse places.

For ten years, he'd lived in war zones before coming back stateside and hiring on with Linus. He cleared his mind and made the drive, planning the whole way.

* * *

SHIT, he was running fifteen minutes behind. He slammed his brakes and skidded to a stop beside Linus' truck and the hangar. The small six-seat plane was just taxiing to a stop. He jumped from the vehicle and jogged toward Linus. The man looked cranky, but that wasn't anything new.

"You're late."

He didn't bother answering. Linus didn't accept excuses and Liv didn't give them. He'd changed his sheets. Straightened up his place and stopped at the store on the way there to pick up more supplies. He lived a simple life. No frills. He had enough for him and not much more.

The door opened, and a man in an expensive suit and designer haircut stepped out first. He snorted as the guy checked his shoes for shit.

Linus stepped forward, and Liv let him take the lead. A small thin figure bundled into a puffy white coat came next. Haskell looked like he was getting ready to trudge through the arctic rather than deal with temps in the mid-forties. The situation wasn't looking good.

"Mr. Grant, I'm Linus Trenton."

He watched Linus hold out his hand, and Mr. D-bag reluctantly shook it.

He lifted his head as two more figures emerged from the plane, an older man and woman. The woman fussed over Haskell like he was a kid. Great, he was babysitting a spoiled brat. Just what he needed in his life, the little shit would probably throw a tantrum as soon as the boy saw his one-room cabin.

"Mr. Trenton. This is out of the way."

"The Sheriff's private airstrip seemed the safest option for the exchange."

Linus turned and motioned in his direction.

"This is Francis Livingston. He's in charge of your client's security while he stays with us."

Suit didn't even glance his way, but that didn't bother him. He studied the interaction between Haskell and the people he was sure were his parents. Paranoia was his greatest asset, and he wanted to get a feel for the enemy, and that was what he considered the client Linus assigned him. He hadn't survived this long by letting people close.

"We'll need to see where Fielding will be staying."

"No," Linus said.

"No?"

Suit's tone conveyed that the bastard didn't get told no often or at all.

"Mr. Haskell's location will be kept secret. You'll be able to contact him through secure channels only. His cell will be kept at our HQ."

"This isn't what we agreed to."

"You hired us to keep your client safe, and that's what we'll do. Now it's after one a.m., and my husbands are waiting for me."

Liv didn't miss the snarl of Suit's nose. He tried not to smirk at the fucker getting ready to piss off the boss. Linus would kill for his men. And Linus had no shame in admitting who he was married to. He'd seen and heard the pride that Linus had for Hunter and Wren. No one could doubt that the three men were a strong triad.

"If you've got a problem you can hop back on that fucking plane of yours."

Liv nearly fist pumped and turned to head back to his SUV. He could go home to his empty, blissfully silent cabin and ignored the world for a few days. It sounded perfect to him.

"Fielding," Suit called for the kid.

The kid held tight to a vintage brown messenger bag that probably cost more than all the clothes Liv owned.

"Fielding, don't disappoint me. Have the script memorized and be ready for table reads and filming."

The kid nodded. Liv's night vision was great, and the kid's features were delicate—slightly androgynous. He wore a thermal hat with long, blond hair sticking out. He didn't look more than eighteen, twenty at the most, even though the file said he was about to turn twenty-three.

"We have an hour drive, let's go."

He almost growled when the parents repeated pretty much the same as Suit. The kid had a stalker, one bad enough it required a security team in another state halfway across the country. All they seemed worried about was some script.

"Don't get fat while you're here. Don't deviate from your exercise or diet plan. We don't have time for you to lose it."

"I said, let's go."

Haskell flinched, but the kid had better get used to him and quick. He motioned for the kid to follow and opened the passenger door. He didn't touch Haskell or try to help.

"Here's his bags. You know the routine."

He took the bags from Linus and stowed them in the back seat.

"Dig in for about a week."

"See you in seven days."

He once again got into his vehicle and made the long ass ride home. The kid was huddled against the door with his head resting on the window. Thankfully it looked like his new charge was going to sleep the whole way. If only he could be so lucky.

WHERE WAS HE BEING TAKEN?

Fielding pretended to sleep, but he was hungry and cold. The last thing he'd remembered eating was a salad that wouldn't keep a toddler full. The guy hadn't even turned on the heat. He hadn't seen much of his new keeper. The guy was all shadowed figure and bad attitude.

Livingston, that's what the guy's boss called him, spoke in guttural tones that reminded him of gravel against stone. No softness existed within it and with the size of Livingston that wasn't much of a surprise. He'd have to tilt his head all the way back just to look at him.

There was something odd about him. Stranger was the fact the interior lights hadn't come on when the doors opened. He didn't think it was a blown bulb, and he sensed it was intentional.

When he was nervous, he talked—a lot, but Livingston didn't invite chatter. So, he bit his lip and pretended to be asleep and thought about the trouble he was in. When the first letter and gift came, he hadn't worried about it. His agent said it was normal to get fan mail. He held onto that belief until the letters from the anonymous fan turned sexual in nature. Outlining all the things anonymous wanted to do to him. It wasn't that they were disgusting in their descriptions. Some of them seemed to be almost romantic. Letters what he assumed a boyfriend would write or assumed what one of those would say. He'd never had one—probably never would.

The break-ins at his apartment spurned the need for a bodyguard. He hadn't anticipated they'd send him to some small town in Georgia.

He was perversely happy about four months away from his agent and parents. It would be like a vacation. His mother put him in his first commercial at two, and from that day forward, his life was always about his big break. Now only four months separated him from his mother's goal. This wasn't the life he'd dreamed for himself, but he kept those secrets to himself. It didn't do him any good to wish for the impossible.

All he wanted was to go to college like other people his age. He wanted a boyfriend instead of the girlfriends his mother always pushed at him. It wasn't like she didn't know he was gay. He'd come out at thirteen. And he was small and femme, as an actor he tempered it to appease his parents and his agent. They didn't care about him beyond his money-making ability.

He must have dozed off because the next thing he knew the bounce of the SUV knocked his head against the window. He straightened and rubbed at his eyes, but he didn't see anything other than trees in the headlights. There wasn't anything else.

"Where are we?"

Nervousness twisted his stomach as Livingston simply grunted. He wrung his hands on his lap and started to fidget on the seat. Suddenly the trees broke into a clearing, and a small cabin stood in the center. As Livingston pulled up, security lights illuminated the yard. Spotlights shined from trees around the perimeter. The vehicle came to a stop.

The man said nothing to him as Livingston opened the door and got out. He followed the man's lead and exited. By the time his feet touched the ground, Livingston already had his bag and was headed toward the house.

He practically jogged to catch up. Lights came on inside.

"Go inside. I have to grab the groceries."

Before he could get a look at the huge man, he was gone again. He left his bag where Livingston had dropped it beside the door. The interior was one big room. A king-sized bed sat angled in the far corner with simple nightstands on either side. A living room area was on the opposite side. The place was masculine, not many personal touches. There wasn't any clutter to be seen. He wondered if the man was just obsessively neat.

He jumped when the door slammed behind him. Livingston passed him and headed toward the small kitchen area. Black cotton stretched across broad shoulders and back. He backed up until the door stopped him, he'd seen big men before. Studios had security guys, but he'd never seen a man this...massive. One of Livingston's thighs was probably as big around as him. This wasn't a good idea. He wanted to go home.

That's when the worst mistake of his life happened, Livingston turned toward him, and he gasped. The exposed skin on Livingston's right side was mottled with discolored scar tissue, and the damage was less severe on his face. Faded somewhat but still noticeable, the worst of them covered his neck and the skin exposed by the short sleeve of the man's t-shirt. The man's eyes filled with rage and Livingston's strong jaw, even covered with a thick beard, he could see it clench in an agitated rhythm. He was caught between horror and pity, the man was...

"Better get used to it now, boy, you're looking at it for the next four months."

"I'm..."

Livingston turned away and ended whatever apology he was going to make. He watched as the man angrily unpacked and put away several bags of groceries. He couldn't move or speak. He hadn't expected, hell, he didn't know what he expected.

"Bathrooms through that door. We're off the grid out here. Everything is run by solar power. I have a mobile hot-spot. Signal ain't the greatest, but it works. I need your phone. It'll be turned off for your stay."

He'd never gone a day without his phone before. There was email. Social media check-in.

"They'll be no arguments. It'll be in the safe."

"Where will I sleep?"

"Don't worry you won't have to share the bed. I have a bedroll. I'll be just fine on the floor. Unless you need something else, I've gotta crash."

One minute Livingston was there, and the next he was gone. He sighed and quickly got ready for bed, he turned his phone off and laid it on the kitchen table. The hardwood floors were chilly under his bare feet. He hurried to the bed and curled up, as tired as he was, all he could do was stare at the ceiling.

He'd screwed up, it wasn't as if he hadn't done it before but for some reason, he still felt the need to apologize. Although, he felt Livingston wouldn't accept it.

Despite the scars, the unmarred side was gorgeous. The dips and peaks of the marred skin fascinated him, and he wondered what the texture would be like under his fingertips. He was a tactile person. He'd always had a bad habit of touching things just to see what they felt like. His parents had told him how annoying the habit was when he was little. His mother claimed he'd rubbed a sore spot from the circles he drew on her arm when she'd put him to sleep as a baby. It soothed him. Although, everyone else thought his touching was an irksome quirk.

The lights flashed off, and he tracked Livingston, dim night-lights illuminated the edges of the room. He could only make out shadows as Livingston snapped open a sleeping bag and arranged it, and a pillow on the floor nearest the door.

He held his breath as the man efficiently stripped down to a pair of boxer briefs. He hoped Livingston wouldn't catch him staring. It was the first time he'd seen a man getting ready for bed.

His parents never let him out of their sight and the only time they left him alone was when his mother was trying to get him a girlfriend to show off.

He used to imagine what it would be like to have a boyfriend. There were plenty of men he'd had crushes on over the years. He'd even worked with another actor when he was a teenager who was about his age who had seemed to flirt with him. Then he'd realized the boy had made it into a game.

He turned over before he got caught. Livingston wasn't exactly happy to have him there. He understood. Who wanted to babysit someone for four months? Even though the space seemed impersonal, he sensed this was Livingston's home, probably his sanctuary and now some stranger was taking up space. Hell, he'd taken the man's bed. He buried his face in the pillow and inhaled, there wasn't any cologne, no scent at all. Livingston must've changed the sheets earlier. He felt stupid for being disappointed. He flopped over onto his back.

When he couldn't sleep, he'd watched TV, but he didn't think Livingston would appreciate him turning it on at almost four a.m. This was going to be the longest four months of his life. He turned his head to find Livingston on his back, with his arms crossed under his head. His eyes widened as the moonlight coming through the windows, leaving Livingston's face in shadows, but shined on the man's powerful chest. One side was covered with thick dark hair, the other side the hair was thinner—patchy in spots.

He slammed his eyes closed and pulled the pillow over his head. He wasn't going to survive his stay there.

THE BOY WAS DRIVING HIM INSANE

Only three days had passed, and he had enough firewood split to last the next few years. With just him, he didn't bother with a fire, but the boy always seemed cold. Fielding wouldn't survive a real winter, and if the kid didn't stop watching him, Fielding wouldn't make the next four months.

It wasn't like the boy complained. Fielding didn't seem to miss the comforts of TV or his phone. Fielding read most of the time. Picked up the cabin even though neither of them made a mess. The boy put himself in charge of meals. That was one thing he wasn't going to fight. Cooking wasn't one of his things.

His phone rang, and he removed it from his back pocket. He answered without checking.

"Livingston."

"Liv, gotta a favor, man."

Favor. Favors for his teammate, Little, were never good. He liked the guy, considered him a friend, but the man just wasn't right. He had some quirks that would make a saint pull out their fucking hair.

"Ya know I'm stuck on babysitting duty."

"Ain't no thing, Liv, I gotta pass my firearm cert per boss man's orders. Ya know I don't carry unless I don't have a choice. But Linus takes this shit too serious."

"It is serious, Little. You know you don't pass the course, he grounds your ass."

"Yeah, Yeah, hand to hand combat I'm the best. My aim just ain't worth shit."

"Wear your fucking glasses, man."

"I don't wanna," Little whined.

He couldn't help grinning. Little was a big ass troublemaker. Didn't take much serious in life but Little loved his job. Linus had threatened to fire Little a few years back, and Little had a panic attack so bad he thought the man was going to have a heart attack.

"I got your back, man, we'll hit the range before I head back to the mountain."

"Thanks, Liv. So how's the kid?"

"Annoying."

"Can't be that fucking bad. You weren't stuck in a van with Raul and Pure for two days."

"ER visit?"

"Fuck, man, it was close. Pure went in pursuit of our runner. Raul was not having that shit. I swear they should just fuck and get it over with."

"We know Raul ain't claiming his boy anytime soon. If I was Raul, I'd have that boy tied to my bed and punishing him for his recklessness."

"Good thing you ain't Raul. Can you imagine Pure submitting to a spanking? I'd pay to see that shit."

"Don't even think about Pure's virgin ass, Raul will kill you for it."

"Ain't that the truth."

"Raul will get his boy without any help from us. He's gonna have his pretty little sub on his knees when the time is right." He turned back to the house to get a cup of coffee and saw Fielding standing there with crimson stained cheeks and a mug held in a shaking hand.

Well, that's what the brat got for eavesdropping on a private conversation.

"Man, I gotta go, I'll give a call when I'm headed in."

"Good deal, Liv."

He disconnected the call and slipped his phone back into his pocket. "That for me?"

"Yes, sir, I didn't mean—" Fielding swallowed hard. "I wasn't listening."

The boy closed the distance between them quickly and thrust the mug at him. He caught it before it made a trip to the ground.

"Black. I noticed you didn't, um, put anything in your coffee. Is it strong enough?"

He hesitated with the mug at his lips. He swore the boy was holding his breath waiting for his approval. Taking a sip, it was perfect, but he took his time to see how long Fielding would keep himself from breathing. Nothing much amused him anymore, but that was doing it for him.

During the time the boy was in his home he'd picked up on little things about him. Fielding's need for approval. The boy's natural submissiveness. Fielding was also downright domestic.

"Not bad."

"I'll do better. Are you going somewhere?"

"No, not for a few more days. We'll head to the office for a check-in, and see what Linus' boy, Hunter, found out about your stalker." Interesting, the stalker comment hadn't earned a flinch, but the moment he said boy, the kid's perfectly arched brows rose. "Make a list of anything you need. We'll hit the store before we come back."

"Can I get candy and chips?"

The question took him by surprise. Fielding didn't look like anything fattening ever passed his pretty lips.

"Do you want candy and chips?"

"So much."

He hid his smile behind his mug at the boy's longing sigh. He'd noticed the boy didn't eat very much, not enough in his opinion, but Fielding wasn't big. Tiny compared to him, probably not for normal sized men.

"We'll see then."

"Yes, sir."

One more submissive little *yes, sir* with averted eyes and the boy was going to find himself on his knees worshiping his cock. He was too old for the boy, but his dick didn't seem to have a problem with it. What made it harder to resist Fielding was a natural submissive born to be someone's boy. He was inclined to dominate and to have the perfect boy in front of him was more temptation than he'd ever experienced.

He needed to get Fielding as far away from him as possible and soon.

* * *

THE LAST FEW days were a level of hell that even eclipsed his worst nightmare, and he was going to make sure it ended. He stowed the boy in the conference room and headed straight for Linus' office. He pushed open the door without knocking not giving a shit what he found on the other side. He slammed the door and strode to his boss' desk.

"He's gotta go."

Linus didn't even flinch simply relaxed back in his chair and stared at him.

"Give him to Pure."

"And why should I do that, Livingston?"

"None of your fucking business, I want him out of my house."

A slow infuriating smirk spread the corners of Linus' mouth, and for the first time in their friendship, he wanted to knock the fucker's teeth out.

The kid's presence was everywhere in his place from Fielding's sweet scent in his bed to meals kept warm in the oven to the boy using his favorite leather jacket as a blanket as he read. It was getting downright domestic at his place. Shit was going to start giving him fucking hives with all the normalcy going on, and he raised his hand to massage the tic under his right eye.

"Want the pretty thing on your dick?"

"Fuck you, man, give him to someone else. I don't care who."

He knew it was a lie, and from the arrogant smirk, Linus picked up on it too. He ground his back teeth together waiting for Linus to call him out on it.

"You know that ain't true, Liv. I send him home with someone else, and you know what's going to happen?"

He didn't want to hear it.

"That's right. You'll ride right over to get your boy."

"You knew this would happen," he hollered.

The man didn't even have to answer. It was right there in his smug expression and the amusement in his blue-green eyes.

He fell into one of the guest chairs in front of Linus' desk and scrubbed his hands over his face. He grew more pissed when his fingers and palm caught on the uneven skin. His wasn't a face or body for permanence. He couldn't even remember the last time he hooked up. He wouldn't admit it aloud, but he wanted someone. Someone who saw the scars yet they wouldn't matter. More than a drunken fuck in a different state or town, where if he were rejected, only strangers would witness it.

"So you still want to send him with Little, Pure, maybe Raul?"

He growled at the mention of Raul being anywhere near Fielding. Raul had tried to fuck Pure out of his system for years, and Raul wasn't picky—he was an any-hole-would-do kind of guy.

"I hate you."

"Want to go a few rounds, maybe show off for him?"

"Fuck you," he rumbled and pushed up from the chair. "Hunter figure anything out?"

"Your boy's stalker is good. His electronic footprint is almost non-existent. He's got a few leads but nothing clear. Probably run into more dead ends. The letters and packages were forwarded through mailing services several times. We're following the tracking info maybe get a geographical profile."

A large Manila envelope sailed his way, and he caught it.

"Burner phone with all of us programmed in. We set him up with a GPS device to wear at all times. There's a drive with all the emails and photos of the letters and gifts, some he's received in the last week. Get to know the enemy. That fucker isn't going to stop. He thinks he owns Fielding."

"Not a fucking chance. Have we considered this could be a woman? I read the file. The verbiage was pretty androgynous."

"It's a thought I had, but my gut says it's a man."

"We won't know shit until we catch them." He tapped the envelope against his knee.

"Go help Little before I put his ass at a desk."

"Still fucking hate you."

He listened to Linus' deep laugh as it followed him out of the room. He slammed the door and went to collect his boy. Either he'd remain strong and resist, or he'd give in, and his boy wasn't going anywhere today or four months from now.

JUNK FOOD EVERYWHERE!

He turned in a circle in the junk food aisle. Chips, cookies, and candy lined the shelves. Livingston told him before they exited his vehicle that they were there for supplies. He twined his fingers so he wouldn't reach for anything. It had been two years since he'd had chocolate. His mother was always there to smack his hand or say something about his weight. He glanced over his shoulder to find the huge man watching him. Livingston's face was expressionless.

The one-sided conversation he'd overheard between Livingston and Little still played in his mind. Spankings, subs, and he wasn't so naive that he didn't know what those meant. He didn't know what a lifestyle like that entailed, but it had made him blush when he'd met Little and Pure, he'd barely been able to talk when he was introduced to Raul. Livingston had mentioned if he was Raul, Pure would be tied up and punished. He banished the ideas before he started blushing and drew attention to himself. His thoughts about Livingston were already more detailed than they should be and he'd only spent a week with the man.

"Did you want something?"

"What can I have?"

"I think one bag of chips, a pack of cookies, and candy will last you until we come back in a few weeks, do you believe that's fair?"

"I can have that much?" He hadn't dared hope for one thing, but he was allowed three different things. He glanced down at the toes of his shoes and tried to hide his excitement.

"I won't abide you getting sick from too much, so we'll discuss how much you can have per day."

"Yes, sir, but could I have two bags of candy instead of the cookies. I never really liked those."

"You may. I'll finish shopping for what we need; then I'll be back."

"Thank you, sir."

Livingston's presence was so overwhelming that he knew the minute the man left the aisle. What was he supposed to get? What if he didn't choose before Livingston was back and he didn't let him get anything. He darted his gaze around, twisted his fingers until they hurt.

"Man, you okay? You look like you're getting ready to have a panic attack." A feminine voice came from his left, and he spun to see a black woman in coveralls watching him.

"He told me I could have chips and candy and I don't know what to get. Maybe if I don't choose he won't let me have—"

"Who's he, and why is he telling you what you can and can't have? That's bullshit."

The anger radiating off the woman made him nervous. He didn't want her to think bad of the big man.

"Livingston doesn't want me to get sick."

"Livingston, that explains it. Come on, little man, let's find you junk food before your Daddy comes back. Uncle Liv can be a bit of an ass, but he's fair. I'm Juvie."

"Fielding."

"Nice to meet you. You're new in town. Liv works quick if he got you already."

He remained silent because he didn't know if it was safe to

explain even to someone who was apparently close to Livingston enough to call him Uncle. He was curious about the big man but refrained from asking questions.

"Okay, why would junk food make you sick?"

"I haven't had it in years."

"No wonder you're too skinny. Princess!" The woman's voice boomed, and a pretty, full-figured girl ran into the aisle.

She wore a flowing hippie style dress that emphasized her curves rather than hid them. She stopped in the aisle, tilted her head to the side, and slammed her hands on her hips.

"You bellowed, Juvie?"

"My new friend Fielding here hasn't had junk food in years. He needs help."

"Oh, hi, I'm Princess. So, what's our budget?"

"Oh, I—I don't know, Livingston said I could have two bags of candy and one of chips."

"Uncle Liv is around. Bossy bastard."

"He's not, he just—"

"Relax, no need to defend him," Juvie assured him.

For the next fifteen minutes, Juvie and Princess helped him settle on chips and his candy.

"Shit." Livingston's voice made him spin, and Livingston was caught in a two-way hug.

It looked as if Juvie and Princess were squeezing the air out of his lungs. He barely kept from smiling, but then he frowned as Princess jumped up and wrapped her legs around Livingston to press kisses to the scarred side of the big man's face. An odd sensation bloomed in his stomach, and he didn't like it.

"Uncle Liv, miss you."

"Princess, you saw me two weeks ago on our last run."

Livingston wore a smile, a real smile that crinkled the corners of his eyes. He wanted that smile for him.

"You don't spend enough time with the Crews." Princess pouted.

Juvie laughed as she peeled Princess off Livingston and hugged Princess around the waist.

"Hands off, Princess, you're making his boy jealous."

"Oh shit, sorry, Fielding. When did this happen?"

"It's a job, Princess, nothing more."

"Oh, so, the allowing him things, but discussing portions is just what you do with jobs now?"

"Princess..." Livingston's tone warned the subject was off-limits.

"Fine, we helped him find things, he thought you wouldn't let him have anything if he didn't choose before you got back."

He felt the weight of Livingston's stare, and he didn't like that it caused him to feel guilty for disappointing Livingston.

"Fielding, is this true?"

"Yes, sir." Juvie and Princess whispered what sounded like Daddy and Livingston swatted at both of them.

"We'll talk about this when we get home."

Princess let out a loud sigh and laid her head back on Juvie's shoulder. "Home, Liv, sounds so...domestic."

"Quit sounding like Linus."

"Bring him on a run with us this weekend. You can't keep him cooped up in that off-grid cabin of yours."

"I'll think about it, but his safety is my main concern, Princess."

"As it should be, but come on, have you seen our Crews? He'll have a helmet on, and no one will know, they'll just wonder about your boy wrapped around you." Juvie's smirk made him nervous, all this made him anxious, and he just wanted to go back to the cabin.

"Can we go home, please?"

"Are you ready?"

"Yes, sir."

Juvie and Princess said their goodbyes and made a run for it in the opposite direction. Princess was grabbing a bag of something from the bottom shelf. He followed behind Livingston as the big man turned and pushed an almost overflowing cart. He tightly hugged the bags to his chest as they approached one of the checkout lanes. His gaze followed the flex and play of muscles under the black cotton of Livingston's t-shirt as the man loaded everything onto the belt.

A small giggle drew his attention, and he darted a gaze to the cashier. The man was pretty, his lashes long and sweeping along the man's high cheekbones. The stranger was watching him with amusement, and he didn't like it. Was the man going to make fun of him?

"Brody, behave, your daughter is just like you."

"Princess filled me in on her way out. He's pretty, Livingston."

"I hate you all. Fielding, put your stuff up here."

"I have money."

"What was that?" The dangerous tone was back in Livingston's voice.

He felt as if he did something wrong but didn't know what. "I can pay for it. I have cash."

"Don't make me repeat myself, Fielding, you won't like the consequences."

Livingston took a step toward him, and he practically threw the bags. It wasn't fear, okay, some of it was fear, but it was something else. He didn't want to disappoint Livingston. The disappointment wasn't the same as what he received from his parents or his agent. This was something else, and he was confused, unsure and yes, a bit scared.

"Liv, you need a lighter—"

"I know what needs done."

"If you say so." Brody gave Livingston the total and the big man paid.

Livingston didn't look at him as he pushed the cart toward the front exit.

"Fielding, here, a present from all of us is in the bag. Good luck."

He frowned as he took the bag with his stuff, but it seemed heavier than it should. He just said thank you and quickened his steps to catch up with Livingston. One peek into the bag, and he stumbled right into Livingston's back.

Strong hands wrapped completely around his upper arms and steadied him.

"Are you okay?"

"They're making fun of me."

"What?"

He turned his head away as he opened his bag and let Livingston see the condoms and lube inside. Livingston's cursing made him flinch, and he started to back away.

"Hey, look at me," Livingston ordered.

No way could he disobey. He raised his gaze to Livingston's face and focused on the scarred side. He tightened his fingers around the bag to stop himself from stroking the uneven and discolored planes. Since the first night at the cabin, he'd fantasized about learning the textures of Livingston's scars. He knew he wasn't allowed to touch, much less think about the action, but it didn't stop him. He wanted, no, needed to know.

"This is the Crews' weird sense of humor. The partners are sometimes worse. Just put it out of your head. It seems they put something else in the bag as well."

"They did?" He lowered his gaze, ignored the offending items and found the bag of suckers he'd thought about getting, but decided on the mini-chocolate bars instead. "I couldn't get those. You said only two."

"It's a welcome to the Crew thing. Now, put your bag in back, and we have to get going, it's a long drive home."

"May I ask you something?"

"One question only."

"Why do you live so far away?"

"It's safer that way."

It was all Livingston said as he took the plastic bag from his hands and tossed it in with the others. The big man led him to the passenger side, opened the door, helped him in and even buckled his seatbelt. He wasn't a child. No, he didn't have any life experience, but he was a grown man. He wished Livingston would notice, but he feared the man saw him as a child and a nuisance. The man might not even be gay. So, he was probably an idiot for his crush, yet it didn't stop him from having one. He stayed silent as his mind twisted in chaotic scenarios of what-if and stupid dreams.

Four months from now, he'd be headed back to a life he hated and leaving the one he was coming to love at the cabin with Livingston. He'd do well to remember that his priorities were a script and making sure he didn't get fat before going back to real life.

JUVIE AND PRINCESS WOULD PAY FOR THIS SHIT

*P*retty, pink and plump lips wrapped around a sucker unconsciously seductive and he wanted to feed his boy his dick. He adjusted his cock behind the zipper of his tactical pants as Fielding slipped the candy from between his pouty lips and licked them. Fielding was curled up on the couch, studying the script cuddled under his leather jacket.

His phone had gone off almost constantly in the two days since their supply run. His nieces thought they were funny. His so-called friends were asking how Daddy was doing. Worse was the package which arrived yesterday from Sin and Saint, and he hadn't even bothered opening it. Those two brats needed more spankings from Pelter. That offending box was stowed in the back of the closet, and it would stay there until he could drop it off to Pelter and make a suggestion about further correction.

He spun back around to finish cleaning his weapon. Inhaled the scent of gun oil. The movements were practiced, ingrained into his memory until he could disassemble, clean, and reassemble his gun with his eyes closed. The familiarity of it normally cleared his mind when his thoughts were veering into dangerous territory.

Thoughts which happened more than he wanted since Fielding

had come into his life and taken up residence in every corner of his home and mind. Years past since he'd thought about his kinks. They were better left forgotten. He'd denied them because he knew he couldn't have a relationship like he wanted. Anyone, even his friends would be horrified to know what was in his head.

"Are you still leaving tonight?" Fielding's timid question had him setting the slide down.

He pivoted on his toes.

"Just for a few hours, there's a takedown, and Linus needs all of us."

"What happens—"

"Nothing will happen. When I leave, I'm putting this place into lockdown. I've already shown you where the panic room is. If something does happen, you go in and lock the door behind you. You and me are the only ones who can open it. Remember, I programmed your handprint into the system."

"Yes, sir, but—"

"No buts, baby. You'll do as you're told, and trust me that I know best. Do you understand?"

"Yes, sir."

"Good boy."

He finished getting ready, slipped his bail enforcement agent vest over his head and secured it. He holstered his weapon in the thigh holster and turned to find the boy staring at him. Fielding's tongue wrapped around the bright red ball of candy. Flicking his cock was out of the question, but that didn't mean it wasn't necessary. The slight pain would rid him of his irritating hard on.

Fielding wasn't even blinking. It was cute and flattering. No one looked at him like that. He couldn't remember a time he'd seen desire aimed his way.

Slipping the chain with his badge on, he waited for the boy to do something, but Fielding kept staring. The boy wasn't even breathing. He wanted to know.

"Breathe."

A long sigh and long, blond lashes fell to half conceal beautiful blue eyes.

He kept his boots rooted to the hardwood floor to keep from rushing across the room to taste the innocence that tortured him. He'd bet what was left of his soul the boy was untouched in anyway, yet that also brought on doubts. Did Fielding's first taste of freedom cloud his naive judgment? Would anybody do especially one as mangled and broken as him? Did the good little boy want to play with danger and run back to safety when it all ended?

His phone rang, and he grabbed it off the counter, connecting the call.

"Yeah?"

"How far you out?" Gage's deep growl of a voice sounded in his ear.

"Forty-five. Just leaving now."

"Get a move on. It seems the guy is in for the night. He scored, and there's a pretty thing on his arm."

"I'll be there, get off my balls." He disconnected the call and shoved it in his back pocket. He closed the distance between him and the couch, he leaned over the back and made the worst mistake of his life. He placed his crooked fingers under the softness of Fielding's pointed chin. The skin was delicate and velvety as rose petals. His boy wasn't even old enough to have a proper beard. He forced the boy's gaze to his. "What are the rules?"

The boy's gaze didn't waver from his mouth. Fielding took a deep breath, and on the exhale, recited the rules he'd established for his boy earlier in the day when he got the call.

"Stay inside. Don't answer the phone unless it's your ring. If I'm scared, I call only you. If anything happens, I'm to go into the panic room. You'll be alerted and will get to me as soon as you can. I'm to eat all the dinner you made for me."

"What else?"

"I'm to behave and to trust that you know what's best for me."

"Exactly. Now, study and I'll be home soon." He released

Fielding too quickly before he gave into the urge to brush a kiss to the candy-stained lips that silently begged for him. How the fuck was he going to make it through without dirtying his pretty boy with all the nasty things he wanted to do to him.

He strode quickly toward the door. His cabin may look rustic, but his security was top-notch. No one got in or out without him knowing, cameras were everywhere inside and out. He could keep an eye on his boy even miles away. He exited and locked down the cabin. Fielding would be safe until he got home. No doubt in his mind about that. It was time to get his head in the game.

* * *

IT WAS ORGANIZED CHAOS, he and Linus were on the front door, Little and Pure were taking the back. As he kicked in the door, the stench of weed, stale cigarettes, and alcohol were overwhelming to his senses even through the bandana around his lower face. He raised his weapon as Linus yelled Bail Enforcement and they cleared room after room. Linus and him worked in perfect sync.

A screech from upstairs would do a banshee proud and a naked man—why did they always have to be naked—stormed out of a room. He dove over the railing just as the fucker compressed the trigger on a shotgun. The wall exploded behind him, and Linus returned fire. He took Linus' Six as their jumper's gun jammed. Linus and him took the steps, and then he had the guy turned over and on his stomach.

The scariest feeling in the world was the cold steel of a barrel pressed to your forehead, and he eased his head up to stare down the barrel of a nine-millimeter Glock.

"Linus."

"I got it. Lady, you want to put that down. We ain't got no issues with you. I'd hate to put a bullet in you."

"Let him go."

"Can't do that, lady."

Any other day he'd laugh and take his chances by knocking the gun from her shaking hands. There was a reason Linus always put him on point or the most dangerous jobs. He didn't care whether he lived or died, and that made him a dangerous man. Not today, he had someone waiting at home—depending on him to come back. It might be a job, but the boy meant more than some damn assignment. A fucked up time to realize it when he was about to have his head blown off by some naked, tweaking woman.

"Want to go home to your boy tonight, Liv?"

Stupid fucking question, and the amusement in Linus' voice showed him his boss and friend knew it. "You damn well know it."

"Don't try anything; I'll shoot y'all." Her voice was hysterical and high enough to break fucking glass.

"Team, make entry at the back. We've got a little problem here."

"Little problem, you ready to make your first family visit, boss?"

"Ye of so little faith, Liv. I haven't made one of those visits in my career. I ain't doing it tonight. Pure, you in position?"

He leaned heavier on the hand holding the fighting man still. He knew what was coming. Pure was the best sniper in the country. Pure was ready with non-lethal rounds.

"On your command, boss," Pure's voice whispered through his earpiece.

"I'll shoot him, I swear." The woman waved her weapon around giving Pure the shot they'd hoped for.

"Take her down."

He reacted and rolled to use the jumper as a shield. The woman screamed as Pure's rubber bullet made contact and two shots rang out as she discharged the weapon wildly.

"We're clear. You doing okay back there, Liv?"

"Get this fucker off me."

"Not your type, huh?"

"Fuck you, man." He cursed as a saggy hairy ass flashed in front of his vision before Linus dragged the guy away.

"Get your ass up from there."

"Nah, man, I'm okay right here a minute."

"Wow, the Death Wish Junkie met his match in a pretty little blond-haired blue-eyed boy, and now he's all cautious and shit."

He opened his eyes to see Linus, Little, and Pure all staring down at him. They wore matching smug grins, but they'd leave Linus to bust his balls. The moment that gun had been pointed at his head, Fielding's sweet face with that lustful expression flashed in his mind. All he could think was that his boy was sitting in the cabin waiting on him and he wasn't going to make it home.

"How the fuck do you do it, man? You got two of them at home, and one pretty thing has me by the short hairs. I ain't even touched him yet."

"Excuse me, you've had him up there for almost two weeks on lockdown and you ain't gotten even a little piece?"

Linus almost sounded disgusted by his restraint. He wasn't led around by his dick like everyone else he knew. He had some self-control—not much, but some.

"I am supposed to be watching him. I thought the point of this being a job was to show some professionalism."

"Dude, I ain't got enough fingers to count off how long it's been since you got laid and you ain't even taste tested the most prime piece to ever fall in your lap."

He was going to kill Little.

"Can I kill him?"

"No, he probably deserves it, but he's the best surveillance man in the country."

"Liv, you do know that the so-called prime piece is as virginal as I am?" Pure asked.

It blew his mind every time Pure talked about his virginity like it was just another thing for a twenty-something guy. Okay, he knew not everyone jumped into bed with every person who asked, but the man was six and a half feet of gorgeous man. He glanced between Pure's spread legs to see Raul standing on the stairs staring at Pure.

Raul was holding onto the zip ties they'd used to secure the couple's wrists.

Raul snarled as he realized he was caught. "We got to get a move on, Jumper's neighbors are gathering on their lawns, and they don't seem like the neighborhood welcoming committee," Raul announced and jogged back down the steps while pushing his charges forward.

He tightened his abs and sat up, then jumped to his feet. It might take a little longer than anticipated to get home. He was going to have to call Fielding. For the first time in his life, he was going to have to call and check-in with someone that wasn't a commanding officer or co-worker.

FIELDING DIDN'T LIKE BEING ALONE

$\mathcal{T}$he cabin was too quiet, Livingston didn't make much noise, but at least he knew the man was around. He moved around the kitchen with the heavy weight of Livingston's jacket hanging on him. He'd grabbed one of Livingston's t-shirts from the laundry he'd folded earlier and even a pair of his socks. The man probably wouldn't appreciate him wearing his clothes. He felt safer than he had in a long time, and he'd even washed with Livingston's body wash and shampoo. He shook the bag of Kettle Corn Popcorn into a big bowl as he listened to the movie's opening credits. Livingston had a surprising collection of movies and not just blood and guts or action ones either. He loved action movies, though, and the hunky leading men, but none of them would ever again compare to the sight of Livingston in his tactical gear.

He'd forgotten how to breathe until Livingston ordered him to. That bossy stuff shouldn't be as sexy as it was, but he couldn't deny that is was. It wasn't just Livingston being dominating. Livingston made sure he was okay. That he ate enough. Slept enough. He felt cared for, and he could almost pretend that he was loved.

He shook his head and cradled the bowl in his arms as he headed back to the couch. He had a few hours to kill. Normally he'd be in bed by now, going at the same time Livingston did. The big man called a few hours ago and said he would be late; the job hadn't turned out as simple as he'd thought. Livingston asked him if he wanted to have someone come and stay with him, but he didn't want anyone else in the house with him. He knew Livingston didn't like anyone else in his space. He'd wanted to ask questions. Instead, he'd let Livingston get back to work so he could come home.

He was chewing the first bite of popcorn just as the beginning explosion toppled a building and he settled in to enjoy the movie until Livingston came home. Leaning his head back, he curled his legs and set the bowl beside his hip. He could get used to this. No auditions. No nagging parents. A place of his own where his parents didn't have a key to get in to try and catch him doing something he wasn't supposed to. They couldn't portion his food out until he was starving.

Except for his dream of going to college like everyone else his age, this was the life he wanted. He sighed and closed his eyes with a smile on his face.

He woke to a feeling of weightlessness, and he partially opened his eyes to see the uneven skin of Livingston's scars. He must still be dreaming. If he was then he needed to take advantage, he nuzzled the odd texture with his nose and inhaled the scent of sweat and the faintness of soap.

"You let the fire go out."

"I'm sorry."

"It's okay, let me get you all tucked in, and I'll get it going again."

"Bad night at work?"

"Nothing for you to worry about. Just a night like any other. Did you eat all your dinner?"

"Yes, and I had popcorn while I watched my movie."

"Any more candy?"

He held onto Livingston as the man tried to lay him down on the bed. A rough chuckle vibrated the big man's chest, and he smiled into the warmth of Livingston's neck.

"No, sir."

"That's my good boy. Now, it's time for you to go to sleep. I have a surprise for you tomorrow."

He released Livingston's neck and stared up at the man's face.

"What is it?"

"It's not a surprise if I tell you."

A roughened hand stroked his hair, then the backs of Livingston's fingers caressed along his cheek. The big man pulled away and then pulled the covers up to tuck them in tight around him.

"I don't even get a hint."

"You can bat those pretty blues at me all you want; I'm not telling you."

The bed dipped beside him, and Livingston leaned over him with his hand flat next to his left hip. He studied Livingston and noticed something different. It was there in big man's eyes. It seemed lighter and happier, the crinkles deeper when Livingston smiled. The same tilt he had become jealous of at Granger's Grocery.

"Well since I was a good boy and did everything you asked, could I have a reward?"

"And what do you think you deserve?"

"I don't know."

"Why don't you scoot over, get comfortable and I'll get in bed with you after I shower."

"Really?"

"Yes, but first I have to clean up."

He turned on his side and scooted to the middle of the bed.

"I see that's agreeable."

He held his breath when Livingston leaned down and pressed his lips to his forehead. He wondered what it would feel like if Livingston kissed him. Livingston's curled fingers slipped under his chin and nudged his head up.

"Breathe, boy."

J.M. DABNEY

He sighed at the order, and he flinched as firm lips pressed to his, and he put his arms back around Livingston's neck. He was suddenly gathered in the big man's strong arms, fingers roughly fisted in his hair. His head was winched back, and he stared into Livingston's eyes. They were dark with emotion and the angles of his face harsh.

The expression scared him, and he attempted to pull back, but Livingston's hold tightened on his hair. He dropped his arm's from around Livingston's neck and placed his hands flat on the powerful muscles of Livingston's chest.

"You don't pull away from me, boy. Do you understand me?"

"Y—yes, sir." Livingston's tightly clenched fist didn't hurt, but he looked angry.

"I'll shower and be right back."

As quickly as Livingston sat beside him, the man was gone. Maybe this was all a dream, and he was still asleep on the couch waiting for Livingston to come home. He stretched out flat on his back and stared up at the ceiling. The shower started, and he peeked toward the bathroom to find the door cracked. He held his breath as he watched Livingston strip. He'd studied Livingston's silhouette in the dark as the man prepared for bed, but it hadn't prepared him for the man in full light.

Livingston was perfection; the extensive scarring didn't take away from the power the man exuded. He pressed his fingers to his lips as he remembered the uneven texture, a combination of rough and soft. Dark, curly hair covered Livingston's left side from collarbones to the waistband of tight boxer briefs. He held his breath and bit his bottom lip as Livingston hooked his fingers in the side of his underwear and pushed them down. His eyes widened at the man's thick cock.

He noticed Livingston tense, and he dragged his gaze up to the man's face. The man looked angry—not like he had a few minutes before—Livingston stared into the mirror. Livingston stroked his hand over the side of his face, lower to his neck and chest. He flinched as emotionless eyes stared at him and the door slammed.

The shuttered emotion and the loud boom of the door caused his chest to tighten. His world was very much about looks and popularity, and he hated it. Evil existed in the prettiest forms, users, and abusers who took without thought of giving anything back.

He wanted Livingston. He feared the intensity of it. For almost twenty-three years he'd only done what everyone else wanted for him, and he didn't want that anymore. He didn't want to go back to life as normal. Nothing waited for him in Los Angeles—just more misery. Could he let himself be selfish and ask for what he needed? Was he crazy to crave the life he'd found here with a man who probably saw him as nothing more than some one-off? A momentary distraction while Livingston had a pretty yet annoying boy around?

He turned over and hugged his pillow to his chest closing his eyes, hoping for sleep before Livingston came back from the bathroom. His neediness embarrassed him, and Livingston probably looked at him pityingly.

SHOULDN'T HE BE USED TO THE STARES?

He'd left the door cracked to let the boy look at him, but once he looked in the mirror, the euphoria of being desired fled. Rage took over, and he'd slammed the door blocking Fielding's view. He raised his hand to stroke his scarred cheek. He knew the texture by heart, the dips of ruined, twisted skin that no amount of plastic surgery would make disappear. Fielding was beautiful, and he was a monster, a perverted beast that wanted to soil the pretty man currently waiting in his bed.

The images of fucking that pretty, virginal body into his mattress caused his cock to harden and his balls to ache. Whatever hard-on he had disappeared as soon as he remembered the lick of flame over his body as his bed burned. The scarves around his wrists and ankles. His screams drowned out the laughter of his mother as she watched him burn. He'd begged. Promised her he'd be good until the agony took his voice.

He didn't remember the rescue or the days and weeks which followed, time lost in a haze of painkillers or pain as they scrubbed his wounds. Infection after infection as his body rejected the skin grafts. Until the night his mother tried yet failed to murder him, he'd thought the bruises and burns were normal. The way a parent showed their love. His evilness needed to be exorcised from him. Punishment was caring.

Thirty years he'd lived as a freak, ostracized for being different. At eight, he'd prayed to the God his mother worshiped to let him die. He promised what was left of his soul to not awake. Instead, he'd learned to hate the body he lived in and when he'd had his first crush on a boy in his school—he knew he wasn't normal. He'd never have what he wanted.

An hour ago, he'd come home to find his boy asleep on his couch wearing his clothes, and he'd wanted Fielding close. Just a moment to hold him, and when his boy awoke to nuzzle his scars, his dick went instantly hard. He'd never had a man look at him with desire, and it was a heady feeling. He needed someone who didn't just want his dick, but him—no disgust over his ruined body and face.

Men always passed him over to go for his better-looking Crew members. They'd bend over for him in the dark, but never kiss or let him touch or want to touch him. He looked down at himself. He was powerfully built with thick, hard muscle from years of serving in the military and law enforcement. He needed to be in top shape. Yet that didn't change his imperfections.

A soft knock drew his attention to the door as it opened and Fielding entered. He didn't say a word as his boy approached and Fielding was his, no matter how much he'd fought it. Fielding's cheeks turned pink as the smaller man slipped between him and the sink. He gripped Fielding's waist and lifted him onto the counter.

"What are you doing in here? You're supposed to be in bed."

"I wanted to ask you something."

"Okay, but then you need to go back to bed while I get ready."

Soft, slender fingertips traced his scars, and he lowered his gaze to the top of the long blond hair. Fielding focused on his chest, traced the dips, and he dug his fingers into Fielding's sides as his boy leaned forward to nuzzle through the hair on his chest.

"I think I should have one of the other guys take over as your security." It killed him to say the words, but he wasn't looking at Fielding as a job—just another client. He'd always acted like a professional, but he couldn't do that with his boy.

Fielding jerked his head up, and he looked down into watery blue eyes. "Why? I've done everything you've told me to. I've been good, sir." Fielding dropped his gaze back to his chest.

He'd thought he'd done away with that useless appendage called his heart decades ago. Always known as the coldest bastard, but during the takedown, he'd worried more about leaving Fielding alone then whether he had done his job or not. He was the best at his job because he'd never had anyone waiting at home—no one to cloud his judgment with sentimentalities.

"I don't want anyone else to watch me."

He took Fielding's head in his hands and tipped his boy's chin up with his thumbs. Tears beaded on pale lower lashes. He bent slightly to sip at the tears, and the saltiness of the drops burst on his tongue. He imagined kissing the tears from Fielding's eyes while he was balls deep in his boy. His resolve to keep his distance weakened as he stepped forward to push between Fielding's slim thighs. He groaned as his hard cock became trapped between their stomachs.

The softness of his boy turned him on, and he hadn't realized until he'd met Fielding how much he'd craved someone soft and sweet—loving. Part of him had secretly yearned for it but denied it. It didn't do any good to wish for things he couldn't have.

"Don't you want to keep me?" Fielding's voice broke as he asked.

"Do you want to be mine until you go back to your real life?" He lowered his mouth to Fielding's and kissed the down-turned corners. Fielding would go back to Los Angeles in a matter of months to the pretty exterior of his life. He had to remind himself and Fielding that some fairy tale happy ever after wasn't meant for them. Permanence wasn't meant for him no matter how much the beautiful boy in his arms made him wish.

Not breaking Fielding was impossible. He'd destroy a part of

Fielding and send him home hoping the young man forgot about him.

"Yes, please."

He was a bastard. "Do you know what it means to be mine?"

"I'll be your boy."

"And what will I be to you?" he asked as he stripped Fielding's shirt off. His boy was perfect. Smooth and flawless except for one tiny ginger colored freckle next to the boy's right nipple. He dropped the shirt on top of his own discarded clothes. "Boy, what will I be to you?" He repeated the question as he wrapped an arm around his boy and lifted him from the counter to work Fielding's pants off.

If it were up to him, his boy would stay naked the rest of his stay. He was going to savor the blatant desire and need he sensed coming off his boy in waves. He dropped the pants and moved back between Fielding's legs, forcing them farther apart with his thighs. He pushed his demons away. All the insecurity and rage he lived with every day. This was about taking something for himself—making memories to last long after his boy left.

"Say it, and I'll give you what you need." He spread his hands over Fielding's back and stroked his boy's soft skin. Counted the delicate vertebrae as he moved upward. He brought his left hand around and raised it to pinch Fielding's chin. He kept his mouth close enough to Fielding's to feel the gentle caress of his boy's breath.

The beat of his heart was a painful rhythm in his chest as the seconds that passed felt like hours as he waited to hear his boy say what he needed him to. It was one simple word—a promise of his submission.

"Daddy, don't make me go."

Soft lips touched his tentatively. The inexperience evident but nothing had ever turned him on more. He hugged his boy tight to his chest. He wouldn't mention the time that would run out.

"I want you to go back to bed while I take a shower. Tomorrow

I'm going to take you somewhere, and we'll talk. Do you understand?"

"Yes, Daddy."

"My good boy."

He tenderly kissed Fielding then helped his boy off the counter. He waited for the boy to leave the bathroom and he gently closed the door with a calmness he didn't feel. Fielding was beautiful. He looked in the mirror at his reflection and studied it for the first time in years. Nothing had changed since the last time. Is what he felt flattery at the thought of a young man wanting him or was it something else?

He'd wanted plenty of men in his life, even had a few for quick, meaningless fucks in the dark or bathrooms. This was different, he knew it in his gut and instinct had saved his ass too many times for him to doubt it. He wasn't going to be able to let his boy go, but he knew he needed to. Keeping Fielding would be cruelty to his boy. He was a broken man who couldn't live in a world like Fielding was used to and he didn't want to. This cabin and his job were his life, but he wanted this one thing even if it would kill him to let his boy go when it was kinder than keeping him.

HE'D NEVER RIDDEN A MOTORCYCLE BEFORE

ielding held tight to Livingston's waist as the wind roared in his ears and they sped down the highway. He'd awakened this morning with Livingston behind him. The bigger man held onto him tight, and he'd felt safe and warm—content for the first time in his life. He'd stayed as still as possible not wanting to wake Livingston and have the moment end.

He was still nervous about what was happening. Livingston had made no promises past the deadline where he headed back to L.A. He knew he had fallen too quickly for Livingston. Was what he felt real or a side effect of his temporary freedom?

When the time came, he knew he'd leave if Livingston told him to go. Until then he'd take what he could get. He ignored the chaos of his thoughts and enjoyed his first ride. The rumble of the motorcycle, the warm strength of Livingston in his embrace, and the heat of the sun.

They'd already ridden for hours, and finally, Liv pulled off onto a dirt road. The path was narrow, and limbs scraped over his leather covered arms. The helmet protected his face. He looked around as he studied the thick trees and greenery. Then suddenly it all thinned to a clearing beside a beautiful, crystal clear lake.

Liv eased the bike to a stop and helped him off. He stood still as Liv removed his helmet and jacket. The day was bright and warm enough his long-sleeved gray t-shirt held off a slight chill.

"That was amazing," he whispered as he watched Liv strip down to his long-sleeved t-shirt but in Liv's customary black.

Liv didn't say a word just studied his face. He wanted to ask what the big man was thinking. Livingston's silence caused unease. Livingston was stoic and quiet, a man who didn't give much away, but he could deal with the man's anger—this calmness seemed unnatural.

"You've never ridden before?"

"No, they always said it was too dangerous. My parents would lose their meal ticket."

"Is that all you are to them, a moneymaker?"

He dropped his gaze to Livingston's chest, "Yes. They've never been physically abusive, but they're not like parents. Managers and guards to make sure I do what I'm supposed to or make sure I don't gain too much weight."

"Doesn't seem like much of a life."

"It's not, but it's all I've ever known. I've always—"

He stopped because he didn't know how to explain. He'd always kept his dreams to himself. He knew they were never going to be more than fantasies he had when life wasn't going his way. They weren't going to come true. Even belonging to Liv had a deadline. When the job was up, they'd go their separate ways, and he didn't know how to make Livingston keep him.

"The rule is complete honesty. You don't hold anything back from me. I can't take care of you if I don't know what's wrong."

"I want to go to college. I want to have friends. I want to eat fast food, candy, chips. I want all the junk food."

"What else?"

"I want what I have here, minus the whole stalker and body-guard thing. No one policing everything I do or think or feel. To never see a scale or a tape measure again. I want a haircut."

"Now, I can agree with all that, but why the haircut, I can't do this with short hair." Livingston growled and wrapped the long strands of his blond hair in his fist and tugged.

He moaned at the slight sting and closed his eyes as the big man nuzzled his throat. He arched his body into Livingston's and the man's thick arm locked around his back to hold him in place. Livingston drew the edges of his teeth down and sharply nipped at his collarbones. He never thought he'd enjoy pain even something as slight as a quick bite.

"Why did you bring me all the way out here?" He was shocked by the huskiness of his voice.

"I've kept you at a distance since I picked you up at the airfield."

"But why?"

"I'm not very nice, little man, or attractive."

For all Livingston's strength, the man had a hint of vulnerability, and he didn't know if he agreed with the not nice part of Livingston's answer. He'd seen the big man with Juvie and Princess, the smiles and the gentle warnings. It was plain to see Livingston's nieces loved him. He wiggled to put enough space between them so that he could see Livingston's face. The scars weren't pretty, but they didn't take away from the handsomeness of the man's features, they added a strange ruggedness to the harsh planes.

"I think you're very attractive."

"How? I'm more scar tissue than skin, boy, I see—"

"But—"

"You're not supposed to interrupt me when I'm speaking."

The tug on his hair was harder and sharper, not the sensual act of before but a small punishment.

"But, Daddy, you're not ugly."

He bit his lip to hide the smile that attempted to turn up the corners of his mouth. Livingston's deep, bass groan was beautiful at him calling the big man Daddy. He still felt a little weird about calling Livingston Daddy and what that meant. His knowledge of sex and BDSM or whatever was limited at best. He knew the mechanics of sex and the prep that went into it.

"And why don't you think I'm ugly?"

He smoothed his left hand up Livingston's chest, drew his fingertips over the textures of Livingston's scars. The dips and twists fascinated him. It was like with Livingston's leather jacket— he loved the smooth and rough material, battered from years of use, but still warm and comforting. Livingston's scent lived in the soft liner and the thick leather.

"I've always liked textures. Certain ones bring me comfort. It's stupid really."

"Not stupid, so explain."

"It's sort of like a security blanket a toddler might have. They find safety in the soft, thickness. It's familiar and right. Calms them. I like textures. Like this." He focused his touch on a particularly silky section between two long twisted ridges. "It's soft like silk, warm. It's real. I've always been touchy. The fabrics and materials of my clothes, some feel perfect, and I'm comfortable, and others are scratchy and harsh against my skin. You feel perfect."

He moved onto the line of Livingston's cheekbone, stroked across it to the slightly misshapen whorl of Livingston's ear. "Can I ask how it happened? Were you in an accident?"

"I was more the accident. My mother lived in a community—" Livingston snorted. "It was a cult. Men had multiple wives...excessive procreation was encouraged."

The big man fell silent, and he simply rubbed at the shell of Livingston's ear waiting for him to continue.

"She wasn't born into the cult like most. She was a runaway, and I guess looking for a place to belong. Before the cult took her in, she was making her way on the streets as a prostitute. I can't blame her for that. Gotta eat, and humans have an innate instinct to survive. She was pregnant, but she didn't know it when she joined the cult. You had to repent for your sins, and she did. She was mindlessly devoted."

A deadness existed in Livingston's eyes as if he wasn't telling a story that was his. He was almost terrified at the calmness.

"She found a husband, shared him with eight other wives, sister-wives. She couldn't have any more kids after me, and women are meant to procreate. She was looked down on, and her so-called husband spent less time with his infertile wife. My entire life she blamed me for it, punished me. I thought that was just the way people showed love. Then when I was eight after she tied me to my bed, she set my room on fire. Stood in the doorway to watch me burn and smiled the entire time. I passed out from the pain. I looked into the case when I got older, read the statements and reports."

"What did they say?" His voice cracked as he asked, he couldn't imagine the hell Livingston went through. The pain and suffering.

"The husband smelled smoke. He ran into the room to find part of the bed engulfed in flames. He threw a blanket over me to snuff out the fire while the sister-wives got the other kids out. He wasn't unkind to me, but he wasn't a father either. He carried me out just as the fire department and ambulances arrived."

"What happened to your mother?"

He loosely draped his arms over Livingston's shoulders. He didn't touch more than necessary. As much as he wanted to soothe away Livingston's pain, he knew one move, and the man would push him away.

"The house burned down around her. Don't do that." Livingston whispered seconds before rough thumbs stroked his cheeks.

He hadn't realized he was crying. It wasn't so much the story Livingston told him, but the tone. Livingston could've been talking about a case he worked.

"She thought if she removed the sin then she'd be healed and her husband would love her. She'd be able to start fresh. Exorcise the demon as it were."

"I don't think you're a demon, and I definitely don't think you're ugly." He needed to see something in Livingston's eyes—some warmth.

"I know what I see in the mirror."

"Did you try—"

"Nothing they can do, all it did was make it worse."

He brought his left hand to Livingston's right cheek. Stroked over the uneven skin with his thumb and loved the tensing of Livingston's body. The man almost pushed into his palm but stopped himself. He wondered what Livingston would be like without all the walls around him.

"Want to take a walk?"

"Yes." He was excited to be out of the house.

The only times he was allowed away from Livingston's cabin was when they'd went to the Trenton offices or the grocery store.

"Keeping you cooped up too long?"

Livingston moved him back, then stood and surprisingly the big man took his hand. Livingston led him toward the small shore, and they started to take their walk.

"No, it was the same at home. Never allowed out without a chaperone."

"Why do you do it then?"

He glanced out over the shimmering surface of the lake and thought about his answer.

"I don't know. It's all I've ever known."

"You're over eighteen; you can do what you want. I'm sure you have the money."

"I don't know about that. I know my apartment is paid for and I always have spending money, my parents have a nice house."

"Do your parents do anything other than managing you?"

"No."

"So, you're paying for them and you."

"Yeah."

"If you want, Hunter can check into your finances."

"Maybe." He'd love to know if he could make a life away from home. The longer he was in Powers, the more he didn't want to go back. He really liked most of the people he'd met, Livingston's Crew, Juvie and Princess, Brody; they made him feel welcomed.

"If you didn't have to go back, what would you do?"

He spun around and walked backward, gazing at Livingston.

"I could do anything?"

"Anything."

He hummed as he thought about what he would do if his life were different. "First, college, I took some online courses, but they said it took away from my job."

"Okay, college, what would you take?"

"I have no idea, but I'd go. I thought about being a social worker and helping kids in foster care, but I don't know."

"Good plan, what else?"

"I'd get a boyfriend."

His smile broadened at Livingston's gruff laugh.

"Out of everything you want to do, a boyfriend would be on the list."

"Yes, it would. I've never had one. Hell, I've never been on a date, not even with a girl."

"What would this boyfriend be like?"

"Um, he'd be gorgeous, tall, dark, dangerous, kind of an asshole."

"So you'd go with one of those bad boy types, go for the nice guys."

"Naw, some of those bad boys have stories to tell, secrets, I've heard some of the stories of the couples and triads in the Crews."

"You have?"

"Little likes to talk just to hear his own voice, so, I got a lot of stories when we went to the office."

"That's one thing Little loves to do. You have college and boyfriend on the list, no travel to exotic places, nothing like that?"

"No, I just want a place I'm comfortable and welcome, a job that I love and someone to share all that little stuff with."

"Not a bad dream, boy."

He grinned as Livingston pulled him back and they continued on. Livingston still didn't say much, but asked questions about him. When it was time to go, he didn't want to leave. It was nice to just be without the act, but he took one last look around.

"Are we going home?"

"Your surprise isn't over with yet."

He cuddled against Livingston's back as they drove out the way they came. He couldn't wait for another surprise.

CLOSE ENOUGH TO TOUCH

 perfect view of the street was framed through the big windows at the front of the Bakery. A shiver of disgust traveled their spine as they took in the scene as bikes roared in the distance then quickly came into view. Five days they'd worked that menial job making coffees and conversation while tempering their loathing of everyone they met. It hadn't taken a lot to get a job working at Decadence Bakery, but they hated every minute of it. Screaming children ran around all the time. Brats by the names of Gunner and Rage, chasing some squealing kid named Mal. The man who owned the place let those filthy things do as they pleased.

They barely kept from snarling as the kids bumped them as the brats moved about. Thankfully, they didn't have to deal with the brats today. Ben, the owner, informed them this morning he'd sent the children to spend the day with his husband, Psycho. They didn't like how the huge man looked at them. Suspicious and all-knowing, no one had a clue why they were there.

They held their breath as Fielding's long, beautiful hair appeared from beneath a helmet. Perfect, delicate features bright and innocent, Fielding's cheeks pink. They strangled a rag in their hands at the sight of that ugly bastard soiling Fielding with his scarred hands.

Fielding would be punished accordingly for letting another touch him, but they had to bide their time. It was perfectly planned, and it couldn't have worked out better. All they'd needed was to get Fielding away from L.A., and they'd succeeded. They were close enough to touch, and soon they'd have him; they'd held on patiently. Why their Fielding was with a bunch of bikers and letting the ugliest of the bunch touch him, they didn't know.

They owned the boy.

"I'm taking a break, if that's okay?" They asked with a perfect smile and waited for Ben to answer.

"You're fine, go ahead. We have another hour before rush hour hits."

"Thank you."

They clenched their jaw at the role of servant. They were better than everyone in this town. Perverts and freaks, unwashed masses that included the boss' husband. Quickly they made their way outside, inhaled the fresh afternoon air.

"Could you bring your asses into the diner, fuck, you can get your boy on your dick later, I'm hungry." A heavily tattooed man they'd learned was named Little, a co-worker of the bastard currently groping Fielding.

"Dude, language." Another of the co-workers, a big guy with a baby face smacked Little on the back of his head.

"Dude, no one is around."

"Get the hell inside."

"Who needs to watch their language now."

"Shut the fuck up, Little, and get inside before I let Pure kick your scrawny ass." The scarred one shoved Little with the arm that wasn't currently around Fielding.

"Ain't nothing scrawny about this hot ass."

The group disappeared inside, the streets weren't deserted but close enough for what they needed to do. They pulled the envelope out of their apron with a gloved covered hand and jogged across the street. It needed to be done quickly. The bikes weren't in clear view of the table the group had taken, and the coast was clear. They dropped the thick envelope on the ground and tucked it under the back wheel.

They moved away, back toward Decadence, calmly looked around to see if someone had spotted them. A slow, smile tugged at the corners of their mouth. Fielding would be theirs—it was only a matter of time.

RAGE IN THE AFTERMATH

*H*e clenched his fists on his thighs and ground his back teeth together. The day started out fine. He'd taken his boy to the lake to get him out of the house, and then out to lunch with his Crew. After that everything went to hell. His job was the only thing in his life he had to take pride in and no matter how empty that made his life seem it was what it was. He'd fucked up, and he should've kept Fielding locked away in the cabin. He squeezed his hands tighter until his knuckles cracked.

"Calm the fuck down, Liv." Pelter's sharp command barely broke through the rage causing the blood to pound in his ears.

The motherfucker was close enough to leave a goddamned note, and he wasn't supposed to be pissed, yeah, fucking right.

"Why wasn't I told that we had a situation?"

"Pelter, we did use your landing strip to bring someone in." Linus leaned back against the long conference table.

None of them wanted to call Camden in on the matter. The big bastard had already arrested them once for going rogue during a rescue to get his over-sized ass out of trouble. The thanks they'd received was being arrested for everything from jaywalking to being questioned for murders old enough to be cold cases older than them.

He darted a glance to where Fielding was curled up in one of the large chairs with his arms wrapped around himself. The misery on his beautiful face broke him. He was meant to keep that young man safe, and he hadn't. Now, the person after him was in Powers. They still didn't have any fucking clues. The note they'd found after they and the Crew had lunch had four words written in block letters. *Close enough to touch.*

"No fingerprints, no trace evidence really. Whoever this person is, the bastard knows what he's doing. How the hell he tracked Fielding down, I'm fucking clueless. We haven't shared a fucking thing with anyone."

"Then let's look at who we have shared information with."

Pelter kept his position leaned back against the wall and Linus pushed himself up to sit on the table. The rest of them took seats wherever. He tugged Fielding close and took the boy's chilled hand. He didn't know what to say to make his boy feel better. The only time they'd ventured into town was today, other than their one trip there for check-in with the team.

"The only people who know are in this room, his parents, and agent."

"What do we know about the agent?"

"Bastard named Grant. Has a taste for barely legal male prostitutes. Nothing stands out in his background check. A lot of high profile clients."

"So, no chance of him being the stalker?"

"I'm not going to say no, but no real evidence."

"What about the parents?"

"Married for thirty years, from all outward appearance perfect couple. Now, look deeper, Mr. Haskell has a girlfriend the same age as Fielding."

He turned to study Fielding's expression, but shock wasn't present.

"You knew?"

"I don't think Father has been faithful a day in his life."

"Have you noticed anyone following you? Maybe paying too much attention?"

"No, not—"

"Daddy?"

He turned toward the door at the sound of Saint's sweet voice to find the young man standing there with his twin, Sin, behind him, and Elisabeth in Saint's arms. Elisabeth wore a tiny flight suit with a patch with her name embroidered on it. They were serious about Elisabeth following in Saint's footsteps as a pilot.

"What's wrong?"

Camden was in movement immediately and had his boys and daughter wrapped in his arms.

"We made the mistake of saying Da was with Uncle Livingston."

As if on cue, Elisabeth started looking around, and he smiled as he stood, Elisabeth's chubby arms reached for him.

"Aw, are your Daddies not treating you right?"

He plucked Elisabeth from Saint as the little girl reached for his face, squeezing his cheeks in her tiny hands. He had a huge soft spot for his nieces and nephews, well, they were really his only soft spot, except for Fielding now.

"Of course my daughter would love your ugly mug."

"Don't hate, Cam, she has great taste." He quipped as he loudly kissed one chunky cheek and then the other, not caring about the slobber the teething baby was leaving on his face and in his beard. Her long, dark brown curls with natural blonde highlights swung around her beautiful face. He carried her back to his seat, he sat with her on his lap, and she bounced and squealed.

"Is that your way of asking if my daughter can sit in on the meeting?"

"I didn't ask, and since she's going to work with us one day—"

"You lost your damn mind. She's going to be a pilot like Ellison."

He was still pissed off, but who could stay mad with so much

69

cuteness. He turned his head as he felt Fielding's cheek against his bicep and the boy was making funny faces at Elisabeth making her laugh.

"Have one of your own and give mine back." Cam made a grab for Elisabeth.

"Children, can we get back to work?" Linus asked.

"I'm not stopping y'all," he answered.

He watched as Cam led his boys to two empty seats and pulled them out, then kissed their cheeks. Cam had run from his boys in the name of protecting them from tying them to someone with a dangerous career. Liv hadn't thought the man would ever give in, but jealousy had taken over. Cam took his usual spot between them. The love the three men had for each other was clear for anyone to see. He tore his attention from them and back to Elisabeth. He held her sides as she bounced.

"What about Mrs. Haskell?" Gage asked without looking up from his tablet.

Gage had taken an active role in the company, but the last few years he was pulling farther away from the action.

Elisabeth curled her arms against her and leaned against his chest. He studied her as she closed her eyes, her long black lashes resting on her rounded cheeks.

"Standing Botox appointments, gym, her financials are boring as fuck," Little whined. "Called a contact of mine, had them do a bit of surveillance for me."

"And we're just fucking hearing about this one?" Linus hopped off the table.

"Ain't costing us anything, I called in a favor for the pretty little man."

"You want to die today, Little?"

"If you're going to kill me, then maybe." Little waggled his brows and blew kisses at Fielding.

His boy giggled. He jerked his gaze toward Fielding and took in the pink of Fielding's cheeks. Jealousy wasn't an emotion he'd experienced in his life. Yes, he envied his friends and sometimes strangers for the things in their life that seemed to come so easy for them, but never like that. No one other than him should even look in Fielding's direction.

He lowered his voice and asked, "Do we need to add to the rules again?"

"Sorry, Daddy." Fielding lowered his gaze to his lap and blushed redder.

"Well, well—"

The crazy man had the nerve to fucking chuckle. He flipped Little off and adjusted Elisabeth until her head rested on his shoulder. Her face buried against his throat.

"Do you want me to take her, Liv?"

"She's fine, Saint."

"Okay."

Sin and Saint curled on either side of Camden as the big man possessively rested his arms over both their laps. All the couples and triads he knew were so open with their love and affection for each other. His mind went back to the conversation earlier about what Fielding wanted. Could he be that person for Fielding? He didn't know if he had it in him to give Fielding everything the boy needed, but it didn't mean that the thoughts weren't torturing him. Yet, he couldn't even keep his boy safe on his turf, and the note was proof of that.

"Little, did your contact find anything useful?" he asked to change the subject and get the meeting back on track.

"Except for his parents being the most boring motherfuckers in existence, not even a fucking parking ticket. I got pictures of old flabby ass in mid-thrust, and you can practically hear the wheezing, but the bored expression on her face is fucking killer—" Little let out a weird maniacal giggle and twisted his laptop around for them to see.

Everyone avoided the laptop screen, and the ceiling became fascinating as hell.

"We're going to have to move Fielding."

"How do you know your location has been compromised?"

Instead of turning his head, he spun the chair so he didn't disturb the baby. "I don't, but to be on the safe side."

"This might be weird, but I got an idea," Pure spoke up from his spot beside Raul.

"You're talking weird when you're dealing with a Crew?" Sin asked.

Laughter filled the room, and the tension eased.

"That is true. This person is obviously obsessed, but from all evidence, they ain't stupid. They cover their tracks even their digital ones, but I'd be willing to bet that their fixation with Fielding would overwhelm their sense of survival."

"And how would we set a trap? Hunter's the best hacker in the country. Cops and federal agents have all been involved. We're more the brute force kinda Crew."

"Not all of us are all brawn and no brains, some of us haven't fried our brains with illegal substances or obsession with dick or pussy."

"Damn, we got our sweet Pure using dick and pussy in the same sentence, and I don't want to hear illegal substance bullshit, who went streaking when we smo—"

"Little, off track."

"Streaking, what the fuck is he talking about, streaking?" Raul growled and turned a murderous glare at Pure.

"Can we get back—"

"I think—"

"Children, get your fucking heads in the game, it's a wonder we get a fucking thing done." Linus sounded disgusted, but the evil mirth in the man's eyes gave him away.

They'd had a bit too much the night of Linus' last birthday. He was well aware of the streaking incident, and Linus was right there with Pure. He tried to forget that night, Hunter, Wren, and Linus going at it later that evening had mentally scarred him for fucking life. There were some things he didn't need to know about his best friends and teammates.

"We kill Fielding," Pure announced like he had said it was raining outside.

It wasn't the idea that shocked him so much it was the fact it was Pure who came up with it. Pure was their most by-the-book member they had.

He raised his left hand and mussed the long strands of Fielding's hair and felt his boy lean into his touch.

"I'm too pretty for jail, so that's all y'all." Little crossed his arms and spun his chair away from the table.

"You just want to shoot something," Linus accused.

"Actually, it's not a bad idea. We have an actor, an experienced sniper, and a top-notch PR guy." Camden sounded too amused by that idea.

"It seems Cam already has a plan, lay it out for us, Pure."

"Like Camden said, we have an experienced actor who I'm sure can pull off a convincing death. We make a very public execution. Fielding will wear a vest. I'll use non-lethal rounds, and we can bring in everyone to brief them on the situation. He can be rushed to the hospital. Gage can hold a press conference announcing Fielding's death and accuse the stalker. The stalker might not believe it, but we've outed him, and there's a chance he'll get sloppy. On the off-chance he does believe it, we can stake out the morgue for the stalker making an attempt to see Fielding's body."

"I repeat, you just want to shoot something."

"I admit to nothing." Pure's expression was too sweet and innocent. "I won't actually shoot him. Three shots near enough for a casual observer to think he was actually hit. A few blood packs with small explosions and we have enough blood to make it look real. There'd be so much chaos and what do people do when shots are fired?"

"They take cover and look for where the shots are coming from."

"Exactly."

"Come with us," Sin and Saint spoke in unison as they swiped Elisabeth and Fielding, leading Fielding out of the conference room.

"Your boys stole mine." He glared at Cam.

"Yours, huh? Does he know that?" Cam asked.

He didn't want to answer, he didn't mind being an asshole, but asshole Livingston had told the innocent Fielding that whatever happened between them wouldn't last longer than a matter of months. He was going to get enough shit when he sent Fielding back to L.A.

"That's my business, now, let's get back to work."

Luckily everyone got their shit together, and they planned, making lists of everyone they needed to call in, but there were few they trusted. He put it all out of his head and set aside his sins to contemplate later.

NOWHERE IS SAFE

Fielding looked out over the street from the break room window. He'd allowed himself to forget the reason he was there for a minute and it was ruined all because of a note. Some obsessive fan who didn't know him but thought he belonged to them. He'd assumed it was a man, but it could very well be a woman, someone he'd passed on the street, and he never knew.

"You're thinking too hard."

He turned and stared at the twins, he knew everyone else could tell them apart, but he'd only met them briefly once.

He must have stared too long because one of them smiled indulgently as the man cuddled the little girl to his chest. "I'm Saint."

"Doesn't—"

"Daddy calls me Ellison. We don't like when other people use our first names."

The same shock he'd felt in the conference room hit him again at the man calling the Sheriff Daddy. It just seemed weird, but he'd done the same with Livingston. Life seemed so much easier before he'd come here. He knew what to expect at home. His life was regimented, days told in spans of auditions, filming, gym, and in calorie counts. In Powers, everyone said what was on their minds. They didn't seem to care what people thought. In a matter of weeks, he was falling for some guy he called Daddy. A man who took care of him and didn't berate him or mentally and emotionally abuse him like every other person in his life had done.

"It freaks you out a little, doesn't it?"

An answer came to him quickly, but he held back to think about it. Was he freaked? It didn't feel like it. Did he find it odd: yes. He took a deep breath before he answered Sin. "I don't know; it just seems odd."

"Does it?" Sin asked.

"A grown—"

"No, listen, it's only odd if people make it that way. Camden takes care of us. Puts ours and our daughter's happiness above his own. All he asks from us is our love and trust. The Daddy thing is really only for at home or when we're around friends."

"Livingston would make an amazing Daddy," Saint announced with a smile.

"Really? Livingston?" Sin sounded shocked by the thought of Livingston taking a Daddy role.

He wanted to defend Livingston but didn't know what to say, so, he just studied Saint as the beautiful man tucked Elisabeth into a sling. Sin approached with a bottle.

"Yeah, think about it, he's possessive, protective, he's sort of an asshole, but he has a major soft gooey center."

He covered his smile at the thought of Livingston being soft. He didn't think Livingston would appreciate it.

"Oh, look, Sin, we got a smile."

He let out a soft chuckle. He didn't have friends, but he wondered if this was what it felt like. People who worried if he experienced happiness or if he was safe.

"I haven't had much to smile over lately."

"Doesn't the whole crazy fan thing just come with being famous?" Sin asked.

"I just thought it was harmless. That's what they kept telling me. I didn't go with my gut and look what it got me."

"Surrounded by hot men with guns who look sexy in their tactical gear. Your life is so fucking hard."

"Okay, that part I'm not complaining about. Livingston makes me stop breathing."

"Daddy in his uniform, the only thing better is when he's naked."

"Saint ain't lying. You should see what happens when Daddy comes home after work. Instant hard-on. We can't bend—"

His face flamed so quickly his cheeks stung, and he dropped his gaze to the floor.

"He blushes." Sin bent to the side in front of him and peeked at his face.

"You all are way too open about sex."

Soft fingertips touched his chin and nudged until he lifted his head to stare into compassionate blue eyes. Sin wasn't mocking him. He relaxed his muscles slowly from shoulders to toes, letting everything flow away at just being with people he could see as friends. It was a nice, comforting thought.

"Sex is great. Like our friend Lucky tells us, it's the most uninhibited act two or more people can do together. It can be making love or something as visceral as dirty, sweaty fucking. It's not something to be ashamed of or embarrassed about."

"I really shouldn't be thinking about sex when someone is threatening me."

"Best time, nothing clears the mind like a hard dick pounding you into a mattress," Sin said with a mischievous grin.

"I'm going back to the conference room."

"No you're not, it's boring in there. We've sat through mission planning. It's all rather boring."

"But, Sin, what if I get to fly the rescue!"

"Ignore my brother; flying is the only other thing that gets him excited."

"I could tell."

Saint had instantly brightened when the man mentioned flying. He didn't know of anything that made him that excited. Life was on auto-pilot for him. He went and did what everyone told him to do, never taking a chance on what he wanted. Unfortunately, the only thing he wanted was to stay there in Powers and maybe have Livingston for himself. That wouldn't happen. Livingston had made himself clear that when this was over, the man would send him home.

The thought depressed him. He'd asked for what he wanted when Livingston suggested assigning him another bodyguard, but that wasn't what this was. He needed to remember that he was there for a short time. When the time came, he'd leave and put on the brave front and pick up the pieces when he arrived home.

"You're too pretty to look so sad," Saint said as he patted Elisabeth through the sling and bounced on his toes as she fussed a bit.

"I hate being pretty."

Sin snorted. "Nothing you can do about it, you're pretty."

"I don't want to be. I just want to be…normal."

"Normal sucks, worse thing in life is to be normal. Carbon copies of the same. Stand out."

"Sin, I don't want to stand out. All I've ever done is be the center of attention."

"Not on your terms, though."

He jerked his gaze to Sin. "My terms?"

"Yeah, your terms. Find you. Crazy shit that makes you *you*. Weird quirks. An over-the-top wardrobe. Be you."

"I don't know what's me. I live by rules…expectations. I can do this. I can't eat that. I can't be me."

"You know what you're forgetting?" Saint asked.

He thought about it, and nothing came to him. "What am I forgetting?"

"You're an adult. You can do what you want. You don't have to act or pretend to be something you're not. Life is about accepting who we are and being happy with it."

"I don't know if I can do that. I've never done anything else. Acting is my job and appearance is all I have."

"Then fix your shit, man, because I'm telling you, you're going to wake up one day fifty and miserable, alone. With nothing to show for it except movie posters and some worthless statues that remind you of all the wasted years."

"Wow, I'm feeling the sympathy."

"I have no sympathy for you."

Sin leaned against him and whispered, "What did you do to my brother?"

"I didn't do anything. He's mean."

"That is a me move. Saint has never done that before."

"Can you tell me what makes me so special, so I can never do it again?"

He warily eyed Saint as he moved around the edge of the room trying to sneak toward the door and safety. He was almost through the door when his escape was impeded. A beautiful older woman with silver-streaked blonde hair was dressed in an expensive suit that did nothing to hide her numerous tattoos and piercings. She looked sweet and kind, but he sensed he was wrong.

"Oh, hi, you're new and beautiful, who do you belong to?"

"No one."

"If that's true, I'm sure it won't be that way long. My boys do love their pretty men. I'm Peaches."

The woman didn't look like someone named Peaches.

"I'm Fielding."

"So, you're Livingston's. A pleasure to meet you. If my Liv doesn't treat you right, just let me know. He isn't too old for me to set him straight."

"Okay."

He didn't know what else to say. She smiled so sweetly, but the menace shining in her eyes frightened him. He did like that she considered him Livingston's but most of the people he'd met called him Livingston's boy.

"Relax, honey; I'm not as scary as everyone may imply. I heard the boys say they're going to kill you in a few days. They seem maniacally excited about an execution. But that's just my boys. Where's my granddaughter?" Peaches demanded as she pushed into the room and held out her hands.

He pivoted in time to see Peaches taking Elisabeth.

"She's so beautiful, y'all did so good."

"Camden does make a pretty baby." Saint's face turned the prettiest shade of pink. "I made the right decision when I asked him to donate."

"When are you having the next?"

"One, Peaches, we've talked about this, and I can't put Lou through that again. It's been nine months, and she still hasn't come to visit yet."

The sadness in Saint's pale blue eyes made him frown because Sin and Saint seemed so happy all the time.

While they were distracted, he took one step out of the break room.

"Stop," Peaches ordered.

He froze at that one word, one foot held off the floor.

"Hold the baby."

A soft wiggling little girl was placed in his arms, and he held her awkwardly. His stomach churned with nausea and the saliva built in his mouth as he fought the urge to puke.

"Look how beautiful she is, babies are—"

"Peaches." Livingston's voice came from behind him, and Elisabeth was easily removed from his arms.

The big man made it look so easy. As bad ass and dangerous as the man appeared to be, Livingston looked so natural holding Elisabeth. Livingston even made faces and kissed her cheeks, blew raspberries on her flight suit covered belly. He couldn't even hold the kid for a few seconds without wanting to throw up.

"What, Liv, don't you want to make your mama—"

"You're not my mama, Peaches."

He didn't miss Peaches' almost invisible flinch, but she hid it so quickly that it could've never happened at all. Peaches called them her boys with such pride in her voice. But the story Livingston told made him understand his reaction. The harshness of his tone.

"Don't be mean. I'll call Lily."

"Now who the fuck is being mean?"

"If our daughter's first word is fuck, you're grounded from Uncle time," Saint warned.

"She loves me; you wouldn't do that to her."

He smiled as Sin and Saint collapsed in defeat.

"We have to get home."

Livingston handed Elisabeth over after he gave her another gentle squeeze.

"Everything planned?" Peaches asked

"We're good to go. Linus is going to bring in a few guys to help with the plan. Gibson is on duty at the firehouse that day."

"You're already corrupting the new Chief?"

"Not my area, talk to Linus, Freddie, and Horace—"

"Those two boys have no sense. How they've survived until now fucking amazes me and you're putting them on a mission?"

"They'll be fine. We need muscle, and they have plenty of those. That's if we can get them out of the woods for it. If not, I have a few others I can call."

Livingston avoided further argument as he steered him from the room and toward the elevator. He was nervous about the plan. The possibility of it being over after a year of uneasiness overwhelmed him with relief, but it also disappointed that his time with Livingston grew to a close.

OBSESSION IS THE NAME OF THE GAME

A week had passed since the meeting, and the plan was as perfect as it was going to get. He'd kept his distance from Fielding as much as he could. Holding his boy as he slept, and the touches and teasing were as far as he'd allow himself to go. That tortured him, but it gave him memories for when Fielding went back to his real life.

Those were experiences he'd never have again. He couldn't reconcile his desire for Fielding and his need to protect his boy from—him. He was too fucked up for innocent Fielding.

He leaned back against the counter in his kitchen and sipped at his coffee, inhaled the strong scent and exhaled slowly. Fielding was curled up in his usual spot on the couch. Was his obsession with Fielding any better than the stalker after him? His brain and body screamed Fielding was his and no one else's. The thought of another man putting his hands on Fielding caused rage to course through his veins.

Tomorrow he'd walk Fielding across the main street of Powers and put the plan into motion. If it worked as they hoped, Fielding would be back on a plane to Los Angeles and away from him.

"I've gained weight since I've been here," Fielding announced without looking up from the script.

"You haven't gained a fucking pound."

"My jeans were tight this morning."

"Come here."

He ordered and knew Fielding wouldn't disobey. He twisted slightly and set his mug on the counter.

Fielding set the script aside, eased the leather jacket from his lap, and stood. His boy made his way to the kitchen and stood in front of him.

Against his better judgment, he grabbed the hem of Fielding's shirt and slowly lifted it, keeping his gaze on Fielding's. His knuckles grazed Fielding's warm, smooth skin. Fielding started to drop his gaze.

"No, you know the rules, don't look away from me."

"Yes, Daddy."

"Good boy. You're so fucking beautiful, and you don't even know it. That has nothing to do with your weight or what size you wear." He removed the soft cotton of Fielding's t-shirt and tossed it aside.

He moved Fielding a few steps away from him. He was at his point of no return. There was no way he could deny himself at least one night of possessing Fielding's body. It was a bastard move, but he craved Fielding's first time.

"Daddy," Fielding said as he moved with the slowness reserved for approaching feral animals.

He wrapped his thickly muscled arms completely around Fielding and tugged him flush to his body. He loved the slim lines of Fielding's frame. The way Fielding fit perfectly against him. His cock hardened.

"Yes, boy?"

"May I have a kiss?"

His chest vibrated with a growl. He loved the needy expression in Fielding's pretty blue eyes. He raised his hand, and his fingertips pushed against Fielding's chin, tilted his head up and back. His boy held his breath as he waited, he drew out the moment heightening the anticipation. His gaze was locked on Fielding's mouth, and his dick hardened against Fielding's soft stomach. He wanted to know what it felt like inside Fielding.

"What's wrong, boy?"

"I don't know what to expect and that scares me."

"Hasn't anyone ever played with you before. Kissed every inch of this beautiful body. Teased your ass with fingers or tongue."

"No," Fielding croaked.

He felt like a bastard at the pleasure he took in the edge of fear and embarrassment in Fielding's sweet voice.

Fielding heavily sighed as his hard mouth came down on Fielding's. He kept the caresses gentle as he nipped and sucked at the curves of Fielding's lips, flicked his tongue to the corners. He sensed the moment Fielding gave in to his control and experience. A faint whimper escaped Fielding, and he tugged him closer. Their chests were pressed so closely together that he could feel the rapid beat of Fielding's heart against his.

His thick fingers fisted in Fielding's hair and winched his boy's head back. He looked down at Fielding's face to find his boy staring up at the ceiling. Part of him wished he could leave a mark—something to prove Fielding belonged to him. That was an asshole Alpha move, and he wouldn't do that to his boy. In the end, he wasn't keeping Fielding, but if he was, he'd mark his boy in a heartbeat.

"Fuck, boy, the things I want to do to you." He growled and ran the tip of one finger down the center of Fielding's chest, over the slight softness of his stomach, and stopped at Fielding's waistband.

Fielding bit his lip as his thumb stroked along Fielding's jaw. Fielding was stiff against him and avoided looking in his eyes. He'd already told his boy not to look away from him, and he wasn't going to repeat himself. He lifted his hand to wrap around the front of Fielding's throat, not enough to cut off his breathing but enough to make sure Fielding brought his attention back to him.

The moment of truth was there and would tell him if he should let his boy go or if Fielding would get fucked.

"Do you want to hear the rules? Be careful how you answer, little man, because if you say yes there's no going back. I will use you how I see fit. I'll gag you with my cock until pretty tears are streaming down your face. You'll take my cock when and where I say. Your ass will be so sore from spankings and fucking until you'll remember me every time you move...sit down. I'll own you, and there's no going back."

Fielding instantly tensed, he sensed the fear, but Fielding's cock was harder against his. A no was all it would take. He may be a beast but no always meant no. Even if he were balls deep, he'd stop the minute his boy told him.

"Do you want to make your Daddy happy, baby?"

Fielding's eyes glazed over and he felt his boy's hard swallow against his palm. His boy nodded, but that still wasn't good enough.

"Now do you want to hear Daddy's rules for his boy? Use your words, Fielding."

"Yes."

"Yes, what? I want to hear you say it."

"Yes, Daddy."

He kept his mouth barely an inch from Fielding's. He'd thought about this for so long, weeks of waiting and being good—doing what was expected. The teasing and touching were going no further than keeping him and Fielding on edge. His jeans were strangling his painfully hard cock. He'd never wanted someone as much as he did Fielding and his lust was inappropriate for the situation. Fielding was under his protection.

"So sweet, untouched. Rule one: No one touches you without my permission, I don't care who it is."

"Yes," Fielding whimpered so sweetly.

He arched his scarred brow and again tightened his hand around Fielding's tender throat.

"Yes, Daddy."

"You're always to trust me to know what's best. I'll ask your opinion, but I get the final say."

"Like with the candy?"

"Yes. You will always be ready to make Daddy happy either with your mouth or ass."

"I've never—"

"I know that, and it's my job to teach you how to please me."

He didn't know what fantasies Fielding had had in the past, but what he wanted to do to the boy wasn't going to be the romantic notions he was sure the boy had.

"I'm going to fuck you and nothing else, do you understand, boy?"

A flash of what he assumed was hurt flared in Fielding's eyes, but he needed the boy to understand the limits—that their time together was limited. There wouldn't be a happy ever after at the end of the road. He lied to himself and Fielding, he wanted to keep the boy, but he wasn't going to be selfish. He put the thoughts out of his head and concentrated on making his boy's first time something Fielding would remember long after he put Fielding back on that plane.

He released Fielding, and he stumbled a bit at the loss of contact. Fielding jerked his gaze to him. The desire glazed eyes made a slow tilt pull at the corner of his mouth.

"On your knees, boy."

Fielding obeyed the command and knelt on the hard, rough planks in front of him. Never taking his eyes off Fielding's beautiful face, he worked his belt free. The clanging jangle of the buckle and the soft slither of leather through denim loops was loud in the sudden silence that was only filled with Fielding's heavy panting. Fielding trembled as he released the button and forced himself to ease down the zipper in slow increments.

Fucking wasn't all about sticking his dick in a hot welcoming hole. It was about the build-up. Fucking or making love began as a mind fuck, a jumble of emotions and sensations. Heightened through anticipation. It intensified the pleasure. A barely-there caress to incite a build toward desperation—a call for something harder and faster. Denial made the final act that much sweeter and intense. Before he finally gave his boy his dick, Fielding would weep and beg to be fucked.

He needed that moment to be stamped forever into Fielding's memory just as he'd always remember. His home wouldn't be the same. Fielding's presence was infused into every corner. No matter what happened in the future, he'd never forget his boy.

It was the moment of truth as he peeled the denim to the sides. He reached in, wrapped his hand around his cock and flinched at his touch on his overly sensitive dick. It was as scarred as he was, he took in the ruined skin on the right side and wondered if it would turn his boy off to see it. He almost commanded Fielding to close his eyes, but he couldn't, he wanted to know everything his boy felt. Fielding was so inexperienced in life that his boy couldn't mask his emotions.

That was why what they were about to do was so dangerous, and still, with the knowledge, he refused to stop.

"You ready to learn how to make your Daddy happy, baby?"

His rough fingers combed through Fielding's baby soft hair. He slowly stroked along the thick length of his cock. Pre-come beaded in the slit. He called on every ounce of control he possessed because he was already too close to cumming. Fielding's perfect white teeth sank into his pouted lower lip.

"Relax," he growled as he gently coaxed Fielding's bottom lip from between his teeth with his thumb.

He applied firm pressure under Fielding's chin and tilted his head back. He caught the darkening of Fielding's gaze seconds before he painted his boy's lips with the tip of his dick. They glistened with his pre-cum, and Fielding was the most beautiful thing he'd ever seen. Fielding on his knees, blissed out with the newness of passion and need. He'd done that to his boy.

His right hand curved around the back of Fielding's neck, massaging firmly with thumb and fingertips.

"Open those pretty, pink lips for me."

Fielding obeyed without question, the thick head of his cock teasingly pushed past Fielding's lips, and he growled at the sensation of soft lips—the wet heat of Fielding's mouth closing around the tip. Fielding tentatively tested the textures, and his dick went harder at the shy caresses and the high-pitched whine. He forgot about why they shouldn't do this or what would happen in the morning; he'd never needed anyone this much.

His eyes closed as he moaned and his head rolled back onto his shoulders as he focused on the pleasure.

He jerked his head up as Fielding started to suck his fat cock. Fielding choked until spit ran from the corners of his mouth—down his chin. Tears slipped from the corners of Fielding's eyes. Fielding's face was red as his boy choked again. His free hand sunk into Fielding's hair and tugged, hard enough so he could cause his boy a slight pain.

"You want to suck my cock, boy; you look at me while you do it."

Fielding's hand came up to rest on his hips.

"I want those hands behind your fucking back. Lace your fingers."

Satisfaction filled him as Fielding obeyed like a good little boy.

"Open wide," he growled.

As Fielding opened his mouth, he thrust forward, and Fielding gagged. He felt the convulsion of his boy's throat. He started a slow, deep rhythm, after a few thrusts he felt Fielding's throat relax.

"Fuck, boy, you're so pretty when you cry."

He stroked one of the tears from Fielding's cheek.

"Now, suck me, boy, make your Daddy happy."

He threw his head back, and he let Fielding do what he wanted. His inexperience was evident, but, fuck, that was sexy as hell to him. Fielding had never sucked cock or bent over for anyone else.

Every first would be his; he'd own them before Fielding left him. His dick jerked in Fielding's mouth every time his boy choked, but his boy kept forcing himself to take more.

His balls started to draw up, and he jerked his boy away, he breathed deep and even until he could bring his focus back to Fielding. He grabbed Fielding's hair and tugged him to his feet. Without thought to being gentle, he slammed his mouth down on his boy's. Fielding's lips were so soft they conformed to his harder, thinner ones. He thrust his tongue into Fielding's mouth and lifted his boy until slender legs locked around his waist.

Blindly he strode from the kitchen toward the bed. His boy cried and clutched at him, but his boy's strength wasn't a match for his, and he tossed Fielding across the bed. His gaze stroked over his boy's torso. His little, tanned nipples beaded, Fielding's skin misted with sweat, and he traced the line of pale, blond hair from his shallow bellybutton to where it disappeared into the waistband of his jeans.

He knelt beside the bed, untied Fielding's shoes and eased them off. His boy's jeans were next, and he quickly had Fielding naked on his bed. He'd dreamed of this since the first night Fielding had come to stay in his cabin.

He'd stretched on his bedroll, he'd closed his eyes, and for the first time in years, his fantasy person was real. His cock had been so hard the entire night he'd barely slept, and he'd glanced toward the bed to watch the boy sleep. Innocent and trusting curled up in his bed.

As Fielding watched him from under lowered lashes, he turned and bent to slide the drawer out, removed the condoms and lube that they'd acquired when they went to the grocery store. He tossed it onto the quilt beside Fielding's hip.

"Turn over. I want you on your hands and knees. Ass in the air, now."

Something primal burned to life in his gut as his boy did as he ordered. The smooth, pale curves of Fielding's lush ass were perfect. He took the soft cheeks in his hands and squeezed, parted them to see the wrinkled, little hole.

Fielding tried to pull away, and he punished him with a hard smack to his right cheek, then another to the left.

"I own you, boy, I can do whatever I want, understand?"

"Yes, Daddy." Fielding's voice was muffled in the covers.

"I can look at what I own."

He pushed his thumb to the tight ass and found almost no give. "Have you ever played with your ass, boy?"

"No." His boy could barely get the word out with his stuttering.

He realized that he was going to need a gentler touch with his boy. Fielding was more innocent than he'd first thought. Young men had toys they played with, but it seemed Fielding hadn't ever allowed himself.

"Don't you have toys at home?"

"No, I didn't—they never let me go out alone."

He knelt on the floor which put him at the perfect height to bury his face between Fielding's cheeks. His tongue stroked over Fielding hole, testing the texture and the firmness. Fielding was so fucking tight. If he weren't careful, he'd ruin his boy's first time.

His boy tensed so much his muscles trembled, and he spanked his boy as he tongued his ass, shocked him out of what he knew was embarrassment. It wasn't long before he caught his boy's moans, noticed the way Fielding pushed back on his tongue. He pushed inside and Fielding's back arched.

His cock was leaking, and he was so hard he hurt, so he surged to his feet and took in Fielding's red, abused skin from the spanking. The spit-slicked hole. He flipped Fielding over, his boy's face was flushed, and his body shimmered with sweat. His boy's slim chest worked up and down with his labored breaths.

"Put your head on the pillows, baby," he said as he picked up the lube and crawled onto the bed, settling between his boy's spread thighs. "Don't be nervous, if something hurts you tell me."

Fielding only nodded, but he didn't say anything about that. The damp head of Fielding's pale dick pressed to his stomach, and he slicked his fingers, then pushed his hand between their bodies. He touched Fielding's hole, felt the resistance as he slowly worked the rim. Fielding whimpered and bucked beneath him as he slowly stretched him until he easily pumped three, thick fingers into Fielding.

He praised him. Told his boy how good he was being. Kissed him softly, sipped at Fielding's full lips as he pushed his boy farther toward the point of no return. When the whines became desperate he sat up, he tore open the condom and rolled it onto his cock. He barely kept from releasing like some horny teenager at his own touch. Fielding watched him. Taking in every inch of him with pupils blown with pleasure. He'd done that for his boy. Someone watched him with an expression he'd only dreamed of on nights he was too weak to ignore his needs.

He added more lube and returned to his spot between Fielding's shaking thighs. He wrapped his hand around the base and pressed his thick head to Fielding. He nudged forward until the tip pushed inside. Fielding gasped, and pain tightened his beautiful face.

"Easy, boy, Daddy will make it all better." He pushed another inch inside. The pressure around the head of his dick so tight he barely kept his eyes from rolling back in ecstasy. "Just breathe and push out. I know it hurts, but I'll make it all better, I promise. Give Daddy your ass. You want to make me happy, right?"

His boy nodded and panted against his mouth.

"Tell Daddy how good he makes you feel."

He felt his boy push out and he sank in deeper, not stopping until he was ball's deep. He kissed the tears from Fielding's lashes.

"Daddy, it hurts," Fielding whispered, and he heard the pain in his sweet voice.

"I won't move until you tell me," he promised and hoped he wasn't lying. His body urged him to move, to pound his boy's ass until he filled the fucking condom.

He couldn't do that to Fielding. His boy was giving him a gift, and he wouldn't cheapen that no matter how much he needed to cum. He felt the second Fielding relaxed and tentatively Fielding rocked his hips, fucking himself onto his dick.

"Can Daddy move?"

Fielding's arms embraced him tightly, and he pressed his mouth to Fielding's as he started to fuck his boy slowly. As he savored the heat and the pressure, his body moved in an unhurried rhythm. He took Fielding's moans into his mouth. Kissed him with reverence until Fielding's short nails started digging into his back. His thrusts became sharper and longer, building until he pounded into Fielding. His boy grunted with each brutal slam of his hips and the entire time he didn't break the contact of their lips.

He opened his eyes to watch Fielding. Found his boy's eyes closed as Fielding cried. He was so close, so he took his boy's hard, slender cock in his hand and jacked him to the pace he'd set with his hips. He lifted to watch as a scream parted Fielding's swollen lips and then he felt the heat of cum spilling over his fingers. He slammed his hips against Fielding's ass and ground out as he spilled his seed into the latex.

Every muscle in his body locked up as he threw his head back, shouting as he began to fuck his boy brutally until his pleasure ebbed away. He collapsed onto Fielding, buried his face against his boy's sweaty throat, and savored the stroke of shaking hands over his back.

He arched his back, framed Fielding's face with his hands and tenderly kissed his face as he brought his boy down until Fielding's trembling subsided.

"Baby, you okay?"

He needed to know he hadn't hurt his boy, that Fielding had been right there with him. The small, sweet smile and eyes shining, eased his moment of anxiety.

"Thank you."

"For what?" he asked.

"I didn't want it to be anyone else but you."

Those words tore at him, made him feel guilty, but he was in complete agreement. He didn't want anyone else touching or loving on his boy either.

"Let's get you cleaned up so we can get some sleep."

Fielding nodded again. He lifted onto his knees and held onto the condom as he eased out of Fielding. He looked at Fielding's abused little hole and stroked his thumb over it—made his boy moan. Reluctantly he crawled off the bed and took Fielding's hand, helped his boy stand. He led him to the bathroom to get him showered and forced himself to take in every detail—he never wanted to forget the night his boy became his.

DEATH IS THE BEST BAIT

a panic attack made itself known as Livingston tightened the bulletproof vest. They'd gone over the plan a hundred times, and still, he wasn't confident in it. Blood packs were taped to the vest with small charges to explode by remote. Pure tried to appear reassuring, but the maniacal glimmer in the man's navy-blue eyes made him nervous. He didn't put it past the crazy man just to hit him with one rubber bullet. They kept telling him death was the best bait in situations like this.

"You have to breathe, baby."

He closed his eyes to focus on the gruffness of Livingston's voice. It was the same tone Livingston used last night as he pushed him closer to the edge. Brought the memory of the first burn of Livingston's fingers as he prepared him. He savored the fullness, the pleasure, and even the pain. His ass and cheeks were still sore from Livingston fucking and spanking him.

Every time he'd sat down the discomfort brought him back, and he didn't want to be there. He wanted to go home. Curl up on Livingston's lap and let his Daddy take care of him. Instead, Livingston was going to walk him across the street, and Pure was going to shoot him with a rubber bullet.

"Why am I doing this?" he asked.

"Baby, you're going to be fine. Pure is the best sniper in the country. We've had our best on this, and this fucker isn't leaving so much as a digital fingerprint on anything. Drawing him out is our only option. He needs to get sloppy and the very beautiful object of his obsession being dead or hurt is a way to do that."

"I know that, but what if Pure misses, it's going to hurt."

"I'll reward you for being a good boy."

"Really, what will I get?" he asked as the scarred side of Livingston's mouth pulled into a smirk.

"What does my boy want?"

"Anything?"

"Within reason, remember it's at my discretion."

"Do I have to answer now?"

What he wanted he knew he couldn't have. Staying there with Livingston to try for something permanent wasn't possible. Livingston made it clear that when they drew the stalker out that he'd let him go.

"I won't push on this one."

He nodded his thanks and Livingston helped him into his t-shirt. He shivered as Livingston's big hands smoothed over his stomach, then settled on his hips.

Pure peeked into the room. "I'm going to get in position. Five minutes." The big man practically skipped out of the room.

He shook his head as Pure disappeared. "Is it just me or is he way too happy about this?"

"Maybe a little. He gets to play with his big gun and not his little one for a change."

He giggled and dropped his gaze. When he'd met Pure, he'd assumed the man was the normal one. That wasn't the case. Raul stepped into the room, and there was the reason he thought Pure was odd. Even though Pure appeared normal to anyone who looked at him, the man was hopelessly in love. Raul was a cold, dangerous man, and Pure was sweet, virginal for fuck's sake.

Then he mentally chided himself because wasn't he just as bad. Livingston was dangerous, cold, and still, he couldn't resist. The moment he saw Livingston, despite the scars and anger, he was drawn to him. It had been mere weeks, and he knew he couldn't go back.

Calloused fingertips slipped under his chin and pushed his head up.

"What's going on in your head?"

"I'm just nervous."

"Lying to me will only earn you correction."

"I don't want to go home."

"I can't offer more, baby, we've talked about this."

He knew it was his imagination that produced the slight sadness and regret in Livingston's voice.

Tears slipped down his cheeks because he'd known Livingston's answer. He should be thankful for Livingston's honesty. Livingston didn't tell him lies to have sex with him. It was his decision to give in, and he didn't regret that he let Livingston be his first. If nothing else, when he went home, at least he'd have the memory to keep him going.

Did Livingston think him too naive and young? Maybe the man didn't think Fielding could love him or anyone could love him. Livingston had his moments of being an asshole, he could be hateful, but everyone had their quirks.

"Let's get this freak show on the road. Pure is getting impatient."

"You need to control your boy more, Raul."

"He ain't mine to control, Liv, and maybe you should take your own fucking advice." Raul's voice had a sharpened steel edge, and the warning in it was clear.

"I'll take care of my boy, and you take care—"

"Finish that, and I'll knock your fucking teeth out."

He tensed at the impending violence and didn't relax until Raul left the room. He wasn't used to violence and anger, around

Trenton Security it was barely leashed, always simmering just below the surface.

"Do you do that on purpose?"

"Raul asks for it."

It was all Livingston said before the big man took his hand and led him out of the break room. Livingston slipped his fingers between his, and a sense of calm came over him. Whatever happened he didn't doubt that Livingston would protect him. He tried not to think about what would happen when they left the building instead he focused on Livingston's touch. The way the big man held his hand as they stepped out onto a public street.

He imagined it was a normal day. He ignored the situation.

"I know what I want for my reward."

He smiled as Livingston brought their joined hands to his mouth and kissed his knuckles.

"And what would that be, boy?"

"Ice cream sundae, a Guinness World Record sized sundae with extra hot fudge."

"Out of everything you could have, you want ice cream?"

"So much ice cream."

The deep bass of Livingston's laughter made him bury his face against the big man's chest.

"You're obsessed. Who was talking about looking fat?"

"But it's ice cream."

"Then you can have all the ice cream you want."

He tilted his head back and smiled up at Livingston. Livingston stroked the back of his fingers down his cheek. "You're so beautiful."

If anyone else told him he was beautiful, he'd cringe at the mention of it. He knew he was attractive. Enough people thought that word was the be-all of flattery. He was supposed to be grateful for it, but to anyone else, it was a shallow compliment and one casually thrown around. Livingston believed him beautiful and didn't consider it an empty attempt at fucking him.

"I'll be okay, right?"

"You'll be curled up in bed tonight with your reward. Just take a deep breath, you do this for a camera all the time. You were born for this role."

"Dying isn't exactly Oscar-worthy."

"Depends on how well you do it."

He stepped off the curb, and according to plan, a series of shots could be heard. One whirred past his ear, and he inwardly cursed. He felt the minute power of the mini-explosions against his chest through the vest. Livingston's big body taking him to the ground knocked the breath from his lungs. He panicked at the inability to take in oxygen. Screams echoed around him. Livingston yelled for someone to call 9-1-1. The events to take place were cemented in his brain, but it felt too real. He fought Livingston, but he tried to hold him closer at the same time.

"Fuck, baby, breath, you're fine. It's all—"

Livingston voiced faded in and out, too much chaos and yelling.

"Fielding, my name is Gibson, you have to calm down. You're sending yourself into a panic attack. Take a deep breath, exhale, repeat for me. I know it's chaotic. I know it's overwhelming, but everything is fine. You're better off than Liv, man, Pure hit him twice."

He opened his eyes to find a man who would make Gods jealous, perfection from his almost translucent blue eyes, squared, stubble-covered jaw to a fitness model body. Holy shit, he knew actors and models who would kill Gibson just out of jealousy.

"Motherfucker, I'm going to take him out," Livingston growled.

"Who me because your man is staring at me because I'm so pretty or Pure for shooting you?" Gibson asked.

He felt the need to laugh but thought it would be inappropriate.

"Both, but you can't help being too fucking pretty. Pure did that shit on purpose."

He needed to calm the situation down. A pissed off Livingston meant the man would start throwing punches. He had a feeling that would ruin the plan. "How did I do, Daddy?"

"Oh, boy, you earned your reward."

"Um, maybe you two could plan to fuck when you don't have an audience?" Gibson spoke quietly then raised his voice. "We need to transfer the patient now."

Gibson should be an actor, the urgency in the man's voice completely believable.

"I've lost the pulse!"

He held still, turned his breathing shallow and forced himself to lay still as he was roughly transferred onto a stretcher.

"Clear the street, but no one leaves without answering questions." Livingston's angry voice almost caused him to flinch as the ambulance doors slammed.

He knew he was alone except for Gibson and the driver, Pure and Little would meet him at the hospital and sneak him out.

"You doing okay now, Fielding?"

He opened his eyes to stare up at the gorgeous smiling man.

"You should be an actor."

"No, I'm good, being fire chief is exciting enough for me. Been awhile since I've worn a paramedic uniform though."

"Was Livingston okay?"

"That beast is perfectly fine. I don't see Pure living much longer though. Rubber bullets or not, that shit had to hurt. Just lie back and relax, once we rush you into the ER you can get up. We already informed the ER staff that it's a police operation."

It was over, at least for the moment, and as much as he wanted his time there to last, he didn't want to have to look over his shoulder. He wanted to be safe. Livingston would make sure he made it out. He closed his eyes and let the anxiety fade away. He'd think about all the pros and cons later, all they could do was wait.

ON THE RUN

*H*e glared at the pouting Pure with his black eye and busted lip. His ribs and chest were sore from where the non-lethal rounds connected with his unprotected skin. Bastard did that shit on purpose, and the man deserved the punishment he received. Raul had tried to take his head off after he'd knocked Pure on his over-sized ass. Camden dragged Raul off, and he didn't give a shit where they were. They'd made it to the safe house they'd arranged.

"You could've hit Fielding."

"Man, I hit what I aim for. Big strong man getting all pissy about a few bruises."

"Only takes one."

Pure scoffed as he grabbed his soda and left the kitchen.

He didn't like being away from his boy, but Linus and Little had Fielding in a second location. No one had made it onto their list of suspects, and Gage was at the hospital handling the public relations nightmare. The other man was also going to stake out the morgue to see if Fielding's stalker tried to get to Fielding's supposed body. They could only hope that the fucker got sloppy and revealed himself, or at the very least, left some clues behind.

"You're jumpy, Liv." Peaches concerned voice came from the doorway behind him.

"I should be with Fielding."

"You know that's a bad idea. The suspect might follow you, and that would lead him right to where Fielding is being held. Convincing job today though."

"But was it convincing enough. It went down perfectly but, dammit, Peaches, all he had to notice is one mistake."

"Are you letting him go, Liv?"

He almost started to pretend he didn't know what she was asking, but he'd known Peaches too long to play her for a fool. She'd take his ass out even when he outweighed her by over a hundred pounds and a foot taller.

"It's a job, Peaches."

"It's not just a fucking job, honey. I've known you almost a decade, and I love you, that's why I'm saying this. If you don't keep that boy, it'll be your biggest fuck up yet."

"I can't keep him. What the fuck do I have to offer? Some off-the-grid cabin. This fucked up body and face to wake up to every morning."

"You're more than some scars and paranoia. I've told you when the right one comes along, they won't judge you for the things you can't change. You survived a horrific incident."

He didn't talk about his mother or his life before the foster homes. No one knew the story in its entirety, and he wanted to keep it that way. He'd learned that Peaches knew every last detail, from where his mother started out to how many surgeries he'd had. He was broken, but unlike his friends and co-workers, all his damage was on the surface for everyone to see. Scars and dead eyes that told a story that still terrified him. The heat of the flames, his clothes and skin burning away quickly but in agonizing slowness. He still remembered the stench of his burned flesh, the sickening sweetness of it.

The nightmares had subsided while Fielding was with him. Yet, he knew they'd come back, and he didn't want Fielding around to see his weakness. The screaming and tears, waking up begging for his mother to save him. Her only answer her laughter still echoing in his head. Her smile was burned into him as deeply as his scars.

"I just can't do it. Fielding has a life and career in California. What the fuck do I have to seriously offer him?"

"Your love, Liv. I've seen the way that boy looks at you. He's been asking for you since they snuck him out of the hospital."

"It's his first taste of freedom."

He hated the lie. He'd seen the truth in Fielding's eyes when he'd looked at him after taking his virginity. It was more than his first freedom. It was the way only someone innocent and untouched by the ugly bits of life could love. He couldn't destroy that innocence completely. He already despised his existence, and he wouldn't survive if he pulled Fielding into his hell.

"But you fucked him anyway."

"I told him fucking was all that I could offer."

"When you take someone's first time that isn't a responsibility you take lightly and the fact you took his virginity knowing you were going to send him home makes you more of a bastard than I thought you were. You have experience and age on your side. You should've left him with that gift to give to someone who's going to be around longer than the time it takes the afterglow to wear off."

He pushed his hands through his hair and pulled until his scalp stung. He didn't regret what he did with Fielding. His boy had cried in his arms. He'd kissed the tears from his cheeks that had been red with embarrassment. The submission and the ecstasy, the perfection of his boy's first time—he'd dissolved his boy to unrestrained bliss. It was a gift he'd cherish, and he didn't care if people considered him a bastard. It was an experience beyond compare of what he had in his past or would have in his future.

"I don't need you to bitch me out."

"You might not consider me your mother, I love you like I do everyone else, and that makes you my son. I love you without judgment or condition. The decision you made doesn't sit right with me, but you're an adult."

He didn't want a mother-figure. He wasn't a stranger to envy. Peaches and Lily embraced all their children, blood and adopted, equally. It was the gentleness of a mother's hand. The purity of a mother's I love yous. All that shit was a foreign a concept, to him, a mother's love was pain, humiliation, and exclusion. Nothing was unconditional in life, he held onto that like a life raft in a hurricane. Because if he started to believe, then he'd crave those things he knew he couldn't have. He didn't want anyone's love.

A mother is supposed to have this connection with their children, but what if something inside him was so beyond repair—evil—that he'd never be truly loved. He'd rather avoid the trap and deny that he couldn't let himself get used to the pretty lies.

"Why?"

"Why what?"

"Do you love me?"

"Because you're deserving. I took one look at you, and you were mine, just like the first time I held Landon in my arms. Looked into his beautiful tiny face and it was like being complete. I didn't give birth to you, but you were always mine even if it took me twenty-eight years to find you."

He flinched as she extended her arms toward him and he felt like a bastard when tears swam in her eyes. She didn't let him get away with it, she stepped up to him and wrapped him in her slender tattooed arms. He couldn't relax, he braced himself for the first blow or cutting word, but all she did was hold him tighter. Rubbed his back in soothing circles and tears burned his eyes. His arms held stiffly at his sides started to move on their own accord, and he held her awkwardly. Peaches raised one hand to rest on his unmarred cheek as soft lips stroked the twisted skin on the other.

"If I could, I'd kiss away every last one, but they make you who you are, Liv. They show the world you were stronger than someone's hate."

"I want to keep him." He admitted the truth to her in a low, barely heard whisper. Afraid that if he said it, the universe would punish him for reaching beyond that which he was entitled.

"Then keep him, honey, hold on tight and love that little man until he can't see anyone else."

"I can't."

"You'll get there, but don't ruin your chance for the greatest thing as humans we can attain—love."

He'd reached his limit, and he pulled back, angrily swiped the tears from his face. He hadn't cried since the night his mother tried to kill him.

"Is he okay?"

"He's good, except he said his Daddy needed to bring him ice cream."

He rolled his lips between his teeth, but couldn't suppress his smile.

"He wants his reward for being good."

"But he wouldn't let anyone else get him ice cream. Are we already setting rules?"

"Yes, he has rules."

"You men and your Daddy complexes. Not that I'm bashing you for it, Gib has heard me yell Daddy plenty of times."

And there was the evil Peaches back in full force. "And I could've done without that visual."

"You, like the rest of my sons, are prudes. Sex is the most natural thing in the world."

"What if people don't like sex."

"Then those people can be happy and healthy with their cuddling and affection or none at all. Shame has nothing to do with sexuality or lack thereof as long as everyone is consenting adults. Giving or taking dick or not taking doesn't define us as humans. Simple affection can be as intimate as a full-on fuck-fest. People are too caught up in expectation."

"Why did you only have one kid?"

"I do, just because I didn't give birth to more than one doesn't mean I'm not a parent to many. Gib learned long ago I was going to take in as many as I could. But to answer why I only gave birth to one, I lost several after I had Landon, and the doctors said it was dangerous for me to try for more."

"I'm sorry."

"Me too. Gib and I always dreamed of having a houseful. Even on our first date, we talked about how many kids we'd have. He told me he didn't care as long as they all were as beautiful as I was. What do you know? We have the most gorgeous kids anyone could hope for."

"You're crazy you know that, Peaches?"

"Honey, the woman you see before you was once a conservative college girl and one day I walked into a tattoo shop to find my future. I might have lost my biological family but what I gained far exceeded the so-called loss."

Even as jaded as he was, Peaches made him hope with a few honest words and no-strings advice. Hope was a drug that many couldn't afford. He'd ignored that promise of something sweeter and gentler, that love most craved. Yes, he wished for it, but was it destined for him? He'd spent too many years keeping everyone at a distance, envying people for what they had. For a brief span of time, he wanted to enjoy Fielding, but having him forever wasn't something he could guarantee himself or Fielding.

He was standing still, but mentally he was on the run.

THEY'D PAY FOR THIS

Morgue. The sounds of the shots still rang in their ears. Those people were supposed to take care of Fielding. What kind of protection did those Neanderthals offer if they allowed one of their clients to die on a public street? They could see the spread of blood across Fielding's chest. Rage traveled along their limbs as they tightened their hand around the syringe in the pocket of their stolen lab coat.

They'd stood in the windows of Decadence. Bile burned at the back of their throat when that disgusting creature lifted Fielding's hand to his mouth. That beast soiled their man. Through the cabin window a few nights before they'd watched Livingston take what was theirs. The scarred bastard using and abusing Fielding had caused the beautiful man to cry. He'd pay for that.

At the hospital, they peeked into rooms. Dropped their head as people passed them in the corridors. The stench of antiseptic and death caused them to snarl their nose. They were about to turn the corner when two of their targets came into view through slightly parted blinds, and they stared into a room filled with gurneys and supplies. They took a few steps and pushed the door enough so they could listen to the conversation.

Hayden Gage. The older silver-haired man leaned back against the wall and the scarred bastard mirrored on the opposite side. The two men spoke quietly. A light flickered on and off, and they listened to the low hum of the fluorescent lights.

"It's been two fucking days, how much longer?"

"Liv, you're getting impatient. We've been on longer stakeouts than this."

"My boy needs me."

"Your boy will be fine." Gage wore a smile which bordered on indulgent.

"I made him promises."

"Ones you're keeping. Want your boy back in your bed?"

Fielding was alive? They'd fallen for a trap—almost. They started to back up.

"Don't you fucking start too. I got chewed out by Peaches. Even Linus tried to pull the fucking boss card with me earlier."

"Man, I'm not the one to give you relationship advice. Just be smart and when it's time, let the boy go."

"That was my plan. I had no intention of keeping him."

They clenched their fists in the pocket of the coat. Fielding wasn't a whore. The ugly bastard took what was theirs, and he would pay. They'd watched that abhorrent brute force himself upon the innocent Fielding and for that Francis needed to suffer.

"I'm headed out."

Gage pushed away from the wall and approached Francis. The slightly shorter man slapped Francis on the back. They moved quickly to hide behind a tall rack and removed the cap from the syringe. Francis stepped out into the hall and watched Gage disappear at the end of the hall. While Francis' back was turned, they struck.

They tightly fisted the plastic until the edges cut into their hand. Lowering their head, they bumped into Francis. One quick jab to the thigh and they pushed down the plunger.

"Excuse me, sir."

They glanced back, recognition filled the man's gaze, and they smiled as Francis attempted to step forward. They quickened their steps.

"Stop," Francis bellowed, he closed the distance, but Francis stumbled.

Fear filled their chest as Francis pursued and just as Francis grabbed them, tried to throw them to the ground but they fought out of the loosening hold. They hit the ground and kicked. The tranquilizer weakened the much stronger and bigger man, but it didn't knock him out like they'd assumed it would.

One solid kick, his head snapped back, and the man went still. They struggled out from under him and crouched, searching left and right, thankful for the emptiness of the lower levels.

Payback within their reach, all they needed was patience and time.

They rushed to Francis' feet and dragged him through a swinging door into a deserted, darkened room. Their breathing was harsh with the exertion of moving the huge man. Killing the bastard would be so easy, one more shot or just slit his throat, but they needed the man. They stared down at Francis and decided killing the man seemed a more viable option. Francis was at their mercy.

The soft echo of steps reached them, and they ducked down as a doctor passed by the large glass. Part of them thankful for the distraction. Francis would run to Fielding, and they'd be there to follow, Trenton Security couldn't keep them away from Fielding— not anymore.

BODYGUARD DOWN

The words that had just echoed through the house brought dread to his stomach. *Possible man down,* it was simply three words yelled by Linus, and he was frozen. Livingston hadn't come for him in two days. They'd told him it was for the best. Livingston was the man assigned to him and the safest bet to follow if the stalker didn't believe their setup.

Once he got his limbs moving, he jumped off the couch and ran toward the front door.

"Is—"

He couldn't finish the question, and Raul grabbed his upper arms.

"We don't know anything yet. Livingston isn't checking in or answering his phone, but it could just be his phone is dead. Don't borrow trouble before we know there is some."

He gave a jerky nod. "What are you all going to do?"

"I'm headed out to check the second location. Hunter is pinging Liv's GPS for a location. That man of yours is a beast, and as long as I've known him, nothing has kept Liv down. I promise—"

"Don't promise what you can't deliver."

He didn't recognize the harshness of his tone. It angered him that Raul tried to placate him. He didn't need that bullshit.

"You've been hanging out with Liv too long. Get back to the living room and stay away from the windows, if someone did try to take Livingston down then they might be searching for your location. Your man is going to be pissed if we don't keep you safe."

Raul pressed a kiss to his forehead, and it felt wrong to have someone else's mouth on him even in as an innocent place as his forehead. He wasn't supposed to let anyone else touch him. He'd obeyed Livingston's rules even if the man wasn't around.

He nodded again and stepped back as the front door opened, Raul and Linus disappeared out of it. Little and Pure herded him back to the couch. Blackout curtains covered the windows.

"Why was Livingston alone?"

"Gage and him have been taking turns at the morgue. He showed up to relieve Gage. They talked for a few. Gage realized he forgot something, and when he returned to the hospital an hour later...no sign of Liv. Peaches went by the other safe house and Livingston wasn't there. No sign of a struggle."

"He's not one to go back on his promise, and he promised to take care of me."

"I'm sure Liv will do everything in his power to get back to you, but we're sure he's okay."

Pure was trying to be assuring, but Little didn't look convinced. He wasn't a child, and he preferred if they just told him what was going on instead of trying to lull him with pretty lies. That made it official; he'd been around Livingston too long.

"Let's play some strip poker." Little ran from the room and came back with a deck of cards.

"Daddy wouldn't like that."

He tried not to laugh as Little seemed to deflate and stuck his bottom lip out. For a huge, scary looking man, Little was adorable. He wouldn't say that out loud, though.

Little snorted in disgust. "You boys and your Daddies."

"Don't lump me in, I have no interest in Daddies or being on my knees."

"That's because you've never had sex."

"I don't need to have sex to say that I don't wish for someone to dominate and degrade me."

He frowned at Pure and sat down on the opposite couch. Then he leaned forward to rest his forearms on his knees.

"Why do you think sex is about being degraded?"

Pure shrugged his massive shoulders and seemed to find something on his laptop interesting. The man zoned out like no one else in the room existed.

"Let's go see if we can find something for dinner." Little grabbed his arm and tugged him off to the kitchen.

He batted Little's hands away. The big man didn't need to be in his space. He opened his mouth to tell Little to stop touching him, and a big hand raised to cut him off.

"You don't have to tell me your Daddy wouldn't like me touching you. Pure needs a minute."

"Is he okay?"

"We give him shit, but he always gives as good as he gets, but personal sex questions make him zone."

"Was he—"

"Unless he wants to share, it ain't our business."

"I took you for an invasive sort."

"Not everyone is who you assume them to be."

That made him frown almost as much as Pure's thought on sex. His paranoia spiked as he took a small step backward toward the door. How did someone find Livingston? If something happened, did a person the team trusted betray them?

"You're more paranoid than I am." Little grinned and looked back over his shoulder, his green eyes twinkled.

Little winked and turned back to staring into the fridge.

"What?"

"You're assuming that a person on the team or a trusted individual ambushed your man. I'm crazy, I admit it, and sometimes I don't like it, but it is what it is."

Guilt assailed him at the hint of sadness that colored Little's voice. He was being an asshole. He knew Livingston just wouldn't leave him. Livingston made a promise to him. He slowly exhaled and focused on Little. It was better than wondering if his Daddy was alive or not.

"We all have our issues. Livingston's sending you home, isn't he?"

"Yes, he was honest with me that it wouldn't last past finding my stalker or when it was time to leave to start filming."

The knowledge that Livingston didn't want to keep him killed him, but he tried to understand.

"Why did you say yes then? You're not someone who gives your ass up just for pretty words."

"Livingston didn't give me pretty words." Livingston made no promises beyond a sexual relationship. He'd admit that hurt, but part of him hoped for something more—that Livingston would hold onto him.

Little pivoted on his toes and stared at him. The attention started to make him uncomfortable.

"What did he give you?"

"What do you mean?"

"Can we talk just between us?"

"Are you trying to distract me?"

"I know you're bordering on panic because Liv is missing, but I really want to know what he gave you, besides the D of course."

He rolled his eyes at Little, and the odd man smirked, waggling his brows.

"You're sex-obsessed."

"Man, if you ain't getting any you'd be sex-obsessed too. My last four dates ditched me before dinner showed up."

"Why—"

"Fielding."

Livingston called his name, and he was barely halfway down the hall before he was in Livingston's arms. He clutched at the big man and Livingston returned the tight embrace. Firm lips stroked his wet cheeks.

"What happened?" His question was broken as he tried to suppress his sobs.

"Someone bumped me during the stakeout. They stuck me. I have to ask you some questions."

"Okay," he answered as Livingston led him to the living room.

Livingston eased him down on the couch, but instead of sitting beside him, Livingston took a seat on the coffee table. Livingston looked pale and his features drawn between anger and something else that he couldn't name. Livingston was so strong and self-sufficient, being taken down couldn't be sitting well with the big man.

"I know we've asked these questions before, but I need you to think. The person I saw before I passed out was maybe hundred-forty-pounds, five-eight, blond hair, androgynous, could be a man or woman. Have you seen anyone—"

"Shit, I think I know who it is," Little yelled.

Livingston jerked his gaze to Little. "What the fuck do you mean you know who it is?"

"Exactly what I said, there's a new guy at Decadence. Well, they are pretty androgynous, so they could be trans. I can't remember what their name is. When no one's looking, they're always snarling their nose. I think Ben said they talked about that their family used to live around here. They came to get away for a while."

"Raul," Livingston bellowed.

"I'm on it. I'll go wake Ben and Psycho up see if I can get a location."

"Why the fuck didn't we hear about a newbie in town. They always stick out."

Livingston's hands were curved around the back of his calves, and his thumbs stroked in small soothing circles. But he didn't know if the big man was trying to calm him or himself.

"Unassuming, probably did enough research to drop some names here and there. We didn't think this person was stupid," Pure answered and started to type away on his keyboard.

"I want to know how the fuck they knew Fielding was brought here, and I want to know now."

"I'll get Hunter and Little on it. I doubt our guy is stupid enough to go back to Decadence." Linus crossed his arms over his chest and rested back against the wall. "Where the fuck you taking him?"

"I got a place, but I want to keep it to myself."

"I gotta know where you're at, Francis."

"Sorry, Linus, where I'm going I can't tell you. It's not just Fielding's ass I'm covering."

"I don't like it."

"You don't have to like it, my boy, my rules."

Fielding's attention bounced back and forth as he watched Linus and Livingston, the tension amping up between the two men. Two alphas fighting for dominance. Observing them, he didn't know how they existed in the same space.

"Your boy, huh?"

"Fuck you, Trenton."

Livingston surged to his feet, fists clenched at his sides and he stood, backing up out of the danger zone. The Trenton team moved in to break up the imminent brawl.

"Don't like the truth, Francis?" Linus asked with a cold smile.

"Knock off the contest of the biggest cock; we got a job to do." Gage pushed between Linus and Livingston. "Liv, go do what you gotta to do, but you know if shit goes nuclear then we need to know where you're at."

"We're going camping."

"Fuck no, Liv, those boys ain't right out there."

"Who better to watch my boy's ass?"

"I hope like fuck you know what you're doing."

"I'm doing what I gotta do."

Livingston stepped back as if he didn't want to give his team an opening to attack him.

"Come on, Fielding, we gotta go."

He didn't question just took the hand Livingston held out to him.

"When those fuckers kill you in your sleep, I'm not going to avenge your death; you got me?"

"Perfectly."

What was going on? Livingston didn't speak to him as he was helped into the big man's vehicle and they drove on into the night toward the man's cabin. Fear and anxiousness twisted his gut as he tried to figure out where his life went wrong.

THIS WASN'T HIS FORTE

Two hours of silence and he didn't know what to say. He was taking his boy into a dangerous situation. His friends weren't right in the head, that's why they lived off the grid in the woods. Neither of them were afraid to get their hands bloody. They relished the pain they inflicted on others. Even though he knew and understood that, he trusted the two men. The only thing he could do was go with his gut, and that told him to get the hell out of town.

This wasn't his fucking forte. Gentling and easing his boy's nervousness wasn't a job he was equipped to handle. Some little fucker had taken him down with ease, and his pride stung, but he didn't want to put his boy in danger over his hurt ego. It wasn't his choice, though. He and his team might bend the rules, yet he needed people who didn't think the rules applied at all.

He stacked the last of the camping gear beside the door and glanced to where Fielding sat on the bed, his slender hands folded in his lap. He strode across the room and crouched down in front of his boy. All he'd thought about as he fought to get his limbs to work was that Fielding was unprotected. He didn't care that his team was with Fielding. Keeping his boy safe was his job, and he'd let his dick get in the way.

"Fielding..." He peeked up at the man's face that was shielded by a fall of soft, honey-colored hair. "I promise I'll keep you safe."

"I know you will, but I'm making your life harder than it needs to be."

He couldn't help but smile—Fielding was way too sweet for him. "My life has been hard since my first breath, and that had nothing to do with you. This should've been a straightforward protection job. We let our egos get in the way."

"I just want it over with."

He took Fielding's face in his hands and leaned forward to press his mouth to Fielding's.

"And it will be soon; I promise you that."

He spoke to him soothingly between soft kisses and tried to ignore that his body and mind screamed for him to take—to own.

"I don't want you and anyone else hurt because of me."

"This isn't your fault, listen closely, boy, you have someone who's mixed up in the head that believes you belong to them. You didn't ask to become someone's obsession. When this is over, you can go home, and your life will go back to normal."

"I don't want normal."

He knew what Fielding believed he wanted. His boy wanted some happily ever after that he couldn't give him. When this was over, Fielding would realize the mistake the boy made by giving himself to the beast. He didn't want Fielding to regret the time they spent together, but he also couldn't allow the boy to think that he was going to keep him. That wasn't a mistake he was going to make. Ruining his boy's life wasn't something he was going to do, but he wanted to give his boy a few good memories—make the time Fielding spent with him a pleasant memory at least.

"I know you're not going to keep me when the job is over. You don't have to—"

He cut off the words with a hard, rough kiss. He thrust his

tongue between Fielding's lips in desperation. Being a bastard was normal for him. He didn't know how to be any different.

Fielding's hands fisted in his shirt, and he broke the kiss, only pulled back far enough to look into his beautiful boy's watery blue eyes. Those tears tore at his blackened and broken soul. It made him wish he was different as impossible as he understood it was.

"Fuck me, Daddy, please."

"Baby boy," he whispered as he started to straighten. He needed to put a safe distance between them. Fighting the grip Fielding had on him, he stood and began to turn away.

"Please, I know it's all you can give me, and I need it. I'll beg." Fielding slipped off the bed and fell to his knees.

He studied Fielding's pretty face as the boy worked his belt loose and had his pants undone, he threw his head back as Fielding took his cock into his mouth.

"Fuck, boy, you know how to make your Daddy weak."

He sunk his fingers into Fielding's hair, the strands silky as they tickled his skin. He groaned as he held Fielding's head still and fucked his fat dick between those plump lips. He hated and savored what he saw in Fielding's eyes. Naming it wouldn't do either of them any good, but he put aside the knowledge that his boy thought he loved him. He couldn't accept it.

He forced Fielding to take his entire length, his boy's back slightly bowed as he choked. He used a thumb to gather a single tear and bring it to his mouth. He tore his boy away from him and threw him on the bed, and then he roughly ripped Fielding's pants down until only his boy's smooth, pale ass was exposed.

He didn't say a word as he jerked open the bedside table, removed the bottle of lube. His patience was at an end. He needed to reassure himself that his boy was alive and all his, he prepped Fielding. The tightness and heat around one finger then four was indescribable. He added more lube to his hand and placed his free one between Fielding's shoulder blades. Minutes or hours could've passed as he pushed his boy to his limits.

His boy cried, whimpered, and clawed at the thick quilt. He pushed forward, the tip of his thumb slipped in, too, beside his fingers. Fielding's hole was reddened and swollen around his hand. Fielding bucked and squeezed trying to push his fist from his ass, but he only fisted him harder and faster.

His cock pulsed and leaked profusely as he used his boy, gave him the pain he knew Fielding needed. He jerked his fist from Fielding's ass and studied the flexing hole that seemed to call for him to fuck it. Fielding's slim body collapsed and his harsh breaths blended with his.

Without thinking, he took his cock in hand, lined up and took Fielding in one sharp thrust. He'd never taken anyone bare, and his boy was slick and hot. His boy was a virgin before him, and he hadn't had a fuck in years.

His weight pressed Fielding into the bed, and he pushed his lips to Fielding's ear.

"Is this what you wanted, boy, your Daddy's fat cock splitting you wide?"

"Yes, Daddy, make it hurt."

"Your Daddy will give you just what you need."

He didn't think or question; he fucked his boy hard and fast. Imprinting on his memory every cry, the saltiness of his boy's tears. The clasp of Fielding's ass around his dick was a silky heat drawing him back in every time he tried to retreat.

The legs of the bed scraped across hardwood. Fabric tore under the pressure of Fielding's nails. He fucked his boy like the beast he was with no thought of care or gentleness. He wanted to fill his beautiful boy with his cum. He required part of himself inside Fielding.

His right hand curved around the front of Fielding's throat, loved the gasp and the wheeze as he squeezed just enough.

"You're Daddy's boy, aren't you?" he hissed as he pounded Fielding's ass.

"Yes."

Fielding screamed, and he felt his lips tighten into a smile as he shifted, aimed for Fielding's prostate, and his boy's high-pitched squeal made his cock jerk. He studied Fielding's face, red and wet with sweat. His boy's mouth opened wide, and his breathing was harsh.

He fucked into his boy's beautiful body. Sweaty skin slapping together. He grunted as he worked his way in and out of Fielding's swollen hole. Thought about how sore his boy would be.

A choked scream and his boy clawing at his hand signaled that he'd made his boy come. He straightened as he took Fielding's hips in a bruising grip and pounded at Fielding's hole.

"Fuck, boy, you make Daddy so fucking happy." He pushed the words through clenched teeth.

The force of his orgasm took him by surprise, and he pushed and pulled, saw cum and lube coating his dick, saw his seed gathering at Fielding's rim. He slammed forward one last time and collapsed onto Fielding, then he fisted his hand in his boy's hair and turned Fielding's head until his lips met his boy's softer ones. He kissed his mouth and the tears and sweat from his cheeks.

"Such a good boy."

"Thank you, Daddy."

Fielding's voice cracked, and he stroked his boy's hair, he loathed to leave his boy's body, but they needed to get ready to go. He eased out and listened to his boy's whimper. Before he straightened, he placed a gentle kiss on Fielding's lower back, peace and regret were an odd combination.

"Time for you to get cleaned up, we need to leave soon."

He helped Fielding stand and then Fielding's arms were around him, a teary face pressed against his chest. Sobs tore at his heart.

"Keep me, Daddy, please."

"I can't, boy, I only want what's best for you and I'm not it."

The words were a bitter lie on his tongue. Every second Fielding was in his life, he wanted to grab onto him and never let go, but he needed to protect his boy even from himself.

WHERE WAS HIS PRETTY AT?

*H*e threw his laptop, and it smashed against the wall, the sound of breaking didn't satisfy him like it should have. The vision of the helicopter taking off from Livingston's place earlier playing in his head on repeat. He roughly pulled his phone out of his pocket, and then he pulled up the app for the GPS locator he'd planted. He couldn't get a location which meant the tracker he planted was found or left behind. Fielding could be anywhere.

They had to come out of hiding sooner or later because he'd grown tired of this town and the game. It was supposed to be so easy. The phone calls he'd recorded told him exactly who would watch Fielding and his research extensive enough to make a cover story believable. A family long-gone from town. Who wouldn't believe someone who just wanted to reconnect with their family roots?

Fielding had always been his since their eyes met ten years ago. He'd kissed those lips once and then the moment was ruined by gossip. Fielding never came near him again. His acting career was over, but he'd never stopped thinking Fielding was his. It was easy enough to make it appear to be a crazy fan.

Now he just needed to find out where his pretty was at, but

being on the run complicated his plan but didn't make it impossible. He just needed to be patient. They couldn't keep Fielding locked away forever.

All he needed was the heat to die down.

His phone ringing made him jump, and he checked the display. He'd thrown away his pre-paid phone after the incident at the hospital. His first thought had been to keep Francis alive, but as soon as he'd looked down at the ugly bastard, he'd changed his mind. Francis should be dead, and he would've been if that doctor hadn't almost caught him. His only choice was to run, and he had.

The ringing stopped then immediately began again.

"Hello, mother."

"Nigel, weren't you and your fiancé supposed to be here by now?"

"We're only delayed. I'll bring him to meet you as soon as I can. How are you feeling?"

He kept his voice sweet, and he smiled, no matter how much the woman disgusted him as long as he smiled she wouldn't notice the change in his voice. His mother had driven his father away. If she'd just been the partner his father deserved.

"I'm well. The doctors are positive that the treatment worked. I miss you, though. You've stayed away so long this time."

"I'm sorry, mother, I assure you I'll be home soon."

"I was so happy to hear that your young man said yes."

"I am too."

"Is he around? May I speak with him?"

He strode across the room to the window and fisted his hand in the curtain, eased it aside slightly to look outside. He'd had to move motels. The new place was as dirty and disgusting, but it fit his purpose for now.

"He ran out to the store. I'll call you on my way there, I promise."

"Okay, dear, when should I tell the staff that you're arriving home."

"I don't know yet. I said I'd call when we left."

"Yes, yes, dear, I think I need a nap. I love you and hope to see you soon."

They spoke a few more minutes, and he disconnected the call. He squeezed his hand around the phone until the edges cut into his hand.

Oh, where, oh, where was his pretty hiding?

WHO WERE THESE PEOPLE?

*A*ll he could see were the scars and the deadness of eyes as he nervously stood and waited for Livingston to get their packs out of the helicopter. The two men weren't overly tall, shorter than Livingston, but their sheer mass was frightening. They didn't approach just simply stood there staring with rifles in their right hands aimed at the ground.

The whir of the blades almost drowned out Livingston thanking Sin and Saint for the lift. A strong hand was placed on the small of his back, and he was nudged forward. He glanced back as Livingston grabbed their bags and he slowly walked forward. The wind died down, and it slowly grew quiet.

"Freddie, Horace, been awhile," Livingston greeted the men, but he noticed Livingston didn't reach out to shake.

"Not long enough."

"You still holding a grudge, Freddie?"

"You took me through four states locked in your fucking trunk, yeah, man, I'm still holding a fucking grudge."

"Murder is a serious charge to jump bail on."

"Justifiable."

"Yeah, I've heard that before, Peaches worked miracles to get that charge dropped."

"Why the fuck are you here?" Horace asked.

He wasn't trained, but even he noticed the tightening of Horace's hand around the butt of the gun.

"My boy is in danger and where better to hide out than in your camp."

"Doesn't look like your pretty, city boy has ever squatted in the woods to shit before. You going to need to hold his hand out in the big bad woods?"

"Horace, quit being jealous my ugly mug got him first."

He shifted nervously as Horace and Freddie looked him up and down with a little too much interest. He stepped closer to Livingston.

"No accounting for fucking taste."

He jumped as back pounding hugs commenced and three booming laughs echoed through the forest. Who were these people? He'd assumed the Trenton team were as crazy as he'd ever come across.

"How the fuck y'all been?"

"Getting fucking old, man, gets harder every year. Feel eighty on some cold mornings."

"Shit, you two are the same age as me. Move back to town and live among the civilized people."

"That shit ain't for us. We do just fine out here. We're almost done with that cabin we've been building."

"You two been working on that for what, two years now?"

"Not much else to do out here and I heard kidnapping a man from town was illegal."

"When has a little something like laws stopped y'all from doing whatever the fuck y'all want to do?"

Horace shrugged his bulky mile-wide shoulders. "I can't deny that, but I kinda like consent."

"Come on, let's get to camp before it gets dark." Freddie turned as he talked and headed off into the trees.

"They're crazy, but they're perfectly safe," Livingston whispered as he bent to pick the bags back up.

He stepped in front of Livingston and followed behind the two men.

"How's the team?"

"Linus is married to a local deputy and a bartender, got kids now."

"Shit, Linus went domestic on us? Fuck, never thought that day would happen, but the two-husband thing I can see though. I bet Lily is loving the grandkids thing."

He kept his eyes on the ground, stepping over exposed roots and fallen limbs. Except for the other men's voices, all he could hear was the sounds of nature. Songs of birds and animals scurrying around in the shadows of the trees.

"Yeah. You know Lily."

"She was up here dropping off supplies several months ago, but never mentioned it. She was trying to get us to leave. What about the rest?"

"Pure is Pure, Little's barely keeping himself alive, and you know Gage."

"Still got that hard-on for that boy he's not supposed to?"

"I think he's given up on that one, maybe, who the fuck knows. I ain't seen Gage go on a date in years now."

He zoned out and walked along as the day was slowly dying. He was sore, he smiled to himself, he'd never complain about Livingston taking him however and whenever he wanted. The upward tilt of his mouth fell at the only painful part. Livingston was going to let him go, and he'd be strong when the time came. The memories would carry him through the lonely times ahead of him. He'd rather belong to Livingston temporarily than not at all.

The forest broke, and they walked into a clearing with three tents that surrounded a fire pit in front of a simple log cabin.

131

"Still got plans for that cabin?"

"Stupid dreams, that's all it is."

"Freddie might be playing it off, but that place is for when they start courting to trick some men into coming up here."

"We've been hiding up here a long time, Liv, I think the time of finding men for ourselves has passed." Freddie didn't glance back as he spoke.

Horace and Freddie leaned their rifles against the side of the porch. He frowned as the two men looked at each other. There was something there, a shared sadness that they felt so oppressively their shoulders slumped.

"Did you warn your boy about roughing it?" Horace asked with a deceptively friendly smile.

Livingston led him to a tent, pulled the flap aside and stowed their bags inside. The man took his hand and helped him sit on a low camp chair around the fire. All three men took the other chairs.

"No, but he'll be fine. Everyone should go camping at least once."

Over the night he listened to stories some that were funny and more than frightened him about being stuck with Horace and Freddie. He slowly relaxed as he studied the two men and recognized a lot of Livingston's quirks in them. One of them or both would look off into space and seem lost for a few minutes before they pulled themselves back from their thoughts. Their loneliness was palatable.

"Your boy is beautiful, Liv," Freddie quietly muttered, but didn't look at him. "You're a lucky man."

Freddie sounded envious and sad, he glanced at Livingston and back to Freddie to find both of Livingston's friends watching him.

"Yes, he is. Y'all will find yours."

"Naw, man, we do just fine with jerking off. Best not get used to men who will run from us, ya know?"

"Freddie and me been alone so long we don't even know what to say to get ourselves a pretty boy."

He jumped as Livingston's hand stroked from his knee to his groin, he jerked his gaze to Livingston's. The man watched him with hunger in his gaze. He shot a glance out of the corner of his eye to catch Horace and Freddie staring before they brought their attention to the fire.

"It's not so much what you say."

"Bullshit, it's all about being smooth and a good looking bastard." Horace's voice was harsh and filled with bitterness.

"If good looking was a factor, you think I'd have Fielding? It's about touching—how you make them feel."

"How do you touch him?"

The longing clear in Freddie's words and his chest tightened with empathy. Wasn't that all he wanted? A chance for love and touch—to belong.

"Like he's mine."

Livingston's gaze held his, and he was helpless, he couldn't look away. The big man took his hand and tugged until he stood, he eased down onto Livingston's lap. Livingston's thick cock was under his sore ass, but he involuntarily clenched as he thought about taking Livingston again. It was never enough.

"It isn't just about fucking. Your focus needs to be on them and their pleasure. Their trust and consent your greatest treasure, but you have to earn it. You let them know you care and you want nothing but to take care of them."

Livingston's lips nipped at his earlobe as the big man's hands slipped under his jacket and t-shirt. He couldn't help it when he arched into Livingston's rough hands on his stomach.

"We don't know anything about being gentle. We're going to bed. We get up pretty early around here." Horace shared a look with Freddie.

Freddie and Horace stood so quickly that he pushed back to

Livingston's chest. They roughly tore the flaps back on their tents and disappeared inside.

"Are they—"

"Undo your fucking pants." The dangerous edge of Livingston's voice had him moving before he could think about it. He was uneasy about the sound of Livingston's tone. He shyly pushed his pants down just enough to expose his ass and kept glancing at the tents.

"You're safe. Daddy will always make sure of that."

He trusted Livingston above anyone else. The broken men who'd disappeared into the tents appeared so miserable. He didn't know why, but he wanted to give them something. Voyeurism was innocent enough. No one else's hands would touch him but his Daddy's.

Livingston worked his own pants undone. He lifted his hips, and the wide head of Livingston's cock was at his hole. He bit off a scream as he was impaled. The burn made him lightheaded. Livingston's dick was slick, but he hadn't even noticed any lube. His ass was on fire. Livingston's teeth bit into his shoulder. His cock rested on his exposed stomach as he rode Livingston.

"Daddy's bad boy likes that people are watching him ride his Daddy's cock. They can look all they want, but who do you belong to?"

"You, Daddy, only you."

"Don't be quiet, let them hear how my dirty boy loves his Daddy's dick."

He opened his thighs as far as his jeans would allow, placed his hands on the arms of the chair and bounced on Livingston's cock.

"Daddy," he screamed as Livingston's hand wrapped around his length and squeezed.

He frantically pushed his jeans down his legs so he could open his thighs wider. Livingston grunted under him, but those weren't the only masculine sounds of pleasure he heard. He forced his eyes open and turned to the tents, the flaps were open, and the two men stared at him, barely illuminated by the fire. He could almost pretend they weren't there at all. Their shirts were gone to expose hairy chest and bellies.

Embarrassment stole through him at what he was doing.

"Let them have something, boy, show them they can have a boy of their own, but you only belong to me."

He couldn't look away from them, looking at one then the other as they stared at him. They worked their dicks in a brutal rhythm, they almost seemed in sync, and he matched his ride to the pace of their strokes. He groaned and whimpered, loud even to himself. He didn't know how he felt about being jerk-off material, but the silent misery that surrounded the two lonely men made him push it aside.

"Fuck, boy, I'm gonna cum," Livingston growled against his ear.

He batted Livingston's hand away from his cock and stroked himself closer and closer. Every muscle in his body seized up as a painful grip slammed him down on Livingston's cock. The heat of Livingston's cum filled his ass, and he screamed as he released onto his thighs. He collapsed bonelessly onto his Daddy's chest, clenching around Livingston as the big man kissed his neck, cheek, and temple. Soothing him with gentle strokes of Livingston's calloused hands.

He couldn't keep the words back, and he didn't even try to stop himself, "Daddy, I love you."

Livingston's strong arms tightened around him to the point he could barely pull oxygen into his lungs. The big man shuddered under him as Livingston buried his face against his throat. He felt the big man's lips move and fantasized that Livingston had said the words too. He lifted his head to find the tent flaps closed and everything quiet except for the nighttime wilderness sounds and the crackling of the fire.

THE CREW WAS GOING TO HAND HIM HIS ASS

*I*t had been a week, they'd gotten into a routine, and it was kind of nice out there. He'd spent weeks out there with Horace and Freddie, so the men had become friends over the years. Their first night beside the fire hadn't been mentioned, and it had been a one-time-only thing. He knew the isolation his friends felt, and he'd wanted to give them something—hope that they wouldn't always be alone.

His friends were like him, scarred by life and mired in nightmares they couldn't fight against. They'd never shared their stories, and he only assumed based on the scars covering the two men.

He'd talked to Fielding about what happened, and his boy understood without having him explain it. No way would he allow someone else to touch Fielding while the boy belonged to him. He wasn't above showing off his boy. Horace and Freddie wouldn't take it any farther than some voyeurism.

His friends weren't his biggest problem. His Crew was going to kick his ass. He'd cut off all contact with them when they'd boarded the helicopter. It wasn't that he didn't trust his team. They were the only men he'd trusted in his life, but he couldn't guarantee that the stalker didn't have surveillance set up.

After the fucker's stunt at the hospital, the stalker had to know they were onto them. Which meant Fielding's stalker was on the run and hiding out wasn't helping them all that much. He glanced toward the cabin where Fielding was helping Horace and Freddie. He bent over, dragged his pack from the tent, and dug out the satellite phone.

He called Linus and hoped the man picked up.

"About fucking time you checked in, where the fuck are you?"

"I went camping."

"I thought you were fucking joking, man. You took your boy out there, are you fucking insane?"

He pulled the phone from his ear and then rolled his eyes. He knew the reaction he was going to get. That's why he didn't mention where he'd planned to go.

"It's perfectly safe."

"Ain't anything safe about them."

"I didn't call to get bitched out, what's the situation?"

He turned the camp chair around and sat down to watch Fielding. His boy was smiling, and he was shocked to find that his friends looked almost happy. Horace and Freddie were even joking around. Maybe he'd get his friends to town one of these days.

"As you probably know, the stalker is on the move. Name's Nigel Rauch, twenty-five, no criminal history, only living relative is a mother who lives in Savannah. But the really interesting thing is Rauch is a former child actor. Washed up at seventeen. Little did some digging and found some buried rumors that Rauch had an unnatural obsession with a few of the actors he worked with."

"Any confirmation?"

"Not that we can find. Family has old money, and my gut says they had enough to make the problems disappear."

"Are we going to let that stop us?"

"You should know me better than that. Shit, we've gone up against richer and more dangerous targets without backing down.

But with him going underground now that we know who he is, we need to give him something to come out of hiding for."

"I know, I don't want to use my—Fielding for bait."

He needed to stop referring to Fielding as his because that wasn't the case. Closing his eyes, he took in the happy and musical sound of Fielding's laughter. He was going to miss that and Fielding's warmth, the way the young man didn't treat or look at him like a monster.

When he'd had his first crush in his teens, he'd fantasized about having a boyfriend—someone only his—and it hurt because he knew it wasn't going to happen. He'd dreamed over the years of not having the scars. That he was normal.

"Liv, are you okay?"

"I'm fine, man, just got shit on my mind, you know?"

"Yeah, I know, but—we've been friends for years, and I'll always have your back. But as a friend, I have to say you need to start putting some distance between you and Fielding. You might be acting all big and bad now, but you're going to get hurt, man. This is too close to what you've always wanted."

"I know that, but I just can't seem to stop. He's so beautiful."

Fielding's I love you repeatedly played in his mind. Someone loved him for the first time in his life, and he wanted to hold on tight. But what the fuck did he know about love? He'd never experienced it in his life. Fielding was his first real kiss. Others had drunkenly done it in the past, but as soon as they felt the scars, they jerked away.

"Then keep him."

"I can't do that either."

"You know we're there for you no matter what, but I really wish you'd consider giving something a go between you two. Do you even see how *your* boy looks at you?"

"How does he look at me?"

"Like you're the best fucking thing to ever happen to him. Like I see Wren and Hunter looking at me, or them at each other. We don't get many chances in life, Liv, just *think* about it."

"I will."

"When are you headed back to town?"

"I think we'll head back tomorrow. Fielding is kinda liking it out here, so I thought I'd let him play with the guys a day longer."

"Play, huh? Didn't take you for a sharer, my friend."

"I'm not, but you know Horace and Freddie don't get many visitors. They're turning uncivilized."

"When haven't those two been animals?"

"True, I'll give you a call when we hit the Powers town limit."

"Come to the office, and we'll work on the next stage of the plan."

"Deal."

He disconnected the call.

"We're keeping him, Liv," Freddie yelled and threw Fielding over his shoulder taking off with him into the woods.

He snorted. "Horace, is he bringing my boy back?"

"Maybe after he gets him naked and into the lake."

Shit, he surged to his feet and took off after Fielding and Freddie. All he saw was Fielding hanging onto Freddie's plaid shirt in a death grip as the insane man laughed his ass off. He truly needed to get these boys out of the woods. He caught up with them just as the trees broke and Freddie was splashing into the water.

Fielding squealed as he was submerged in the cold water and his boy was cussing, pounding on Freddie's back as they came back up for air.

"Ain't seen Freddie that happy in years, man."

"He's mine."

"We know that. We don't poach, but Freddie pretends something fierce about being happy out here."

"Why don't y'all come back to town?"

"Too many people. Chaos. Noise. We do okay out here."

"You two can do better than okay."

"We know that too, but—"

"It isn't my business."

Freddie and Fielding splashed around, laughing, and he thought it was nice that he could give his friends a little something to get them through the bad times. He knew memories of Fielding would do that for him in the years to come.

"We've done a lot of bad shit over the years, before we even knew something was wrong with it. It wasn't a bad foster home, our foster mom was kinda cool, but when she hooked up with that old man of hers. It was hell, we just, we're broken, Liv, ain't nothing redeemable about us."

"You have seen the Crews hook up over the years, several of them didn't think they were redeemable either."

"Yeah, you know we kinda hang back, don't try to make waves, but we see a lot. If you don't keep that boy, you're a fucking moron."

"I won't deny that, but do I want to shackle that beautiful and carefree boy to me for the rest of his life?"

"You so fucking do. You going to let them play a little longer?"

"Like you said, Freddie ain't been happy, let him have his fun."

"Thanks, man, my best friend needs more than my cranky ass to keep him company."

Horace gave him a hard slap on the back and then shoved his hands in his pockets.

Later he'd ask about the Rauch guy and what Fielding knew about him—especially find out why the guy would have a thing for Fielding.

He stood back as he watched Horace walk to the water's edge. He saw too much of himself in Horace and Freddie—the two men reminded him of how empty his life was. At the end of the day, all he had was land and a job he loved, one that could get him killed every day. Before Fielding, all he'd thought about was dying, and he'd done it so long he'd never learned how to live.

FIELDING WOULD BE HIS FINALLY

*H*e adjusted his black wig over his dark brown hair; he'd thrown the long blond one out after the incident at the hospital. The heat had died down, and he'd caught sight of Fielding and Livingston entering Trenton Security the day before. He was growing impatient. Nothing about his plan was working the way it should have. It was supposed to be so simple.

They were mindless brutes. Ugly and uncivilized, and they were outsmarting him, and he couldn't allow that to continue. He'd switched out his clothes for more masculine and less androgynous, threw away his makeup and prosthetics. Years in the entertainment industry had its perks. He could make himself look like anyone he wanted, and even his mother wouldn't recognize him. He'd tested out his skills on her several times.

He'd scrubbed himself down with bleach the other night he'd come back to the motel from Brawlers. Little was the weakest target, and he'd used it to his advantage. A bit of attention and flattery, the man couldn't keep it in his pants. It had disgusted him to have that man's hands on him, but he'd established contact, and that's what he needed. He'd walk right into Trenton Security and walk out with Fielding.

The syringe was hidden in his jacket pocket, not enough to incapacitate but enough to make the man compliant. He checked both ways before he jogged across the street. Opening the door, he stepped inside. An empty reception desk filled the small waiting room.

"Hello, how can I help you?"

He turned to find the woman named Peaches standing there. He'd done his research, and she was as abhorrent as the rest of them.

"Yes, ma'am, I'm Nathan, I met Little at Brawlers the other night. He told me I should come by and see him sometime."

"My boys do have great taste. He's in a meeting, but I'll take you to the break room. Do you have time to wait?"

"Yes, ma'am."

"Stop with the ma'am bullshit, call me Peaches. Please, come with me. I'll drop you off and head to the meeting myself. We shouldn't be too long."

"That's great, Peaches, thank you."

He watched as Peaches waved a card over a reader on a panel next to the elevator. That might be an issue if he needed one to get out. He strode to the elevator, stepped inside, and kept himself calm. It was almost over. He'd found the perfect place to hide Fielding until he could take him home.

"I think Fielding is in the break room. I'm sure he can keep you company."

He tried not to appear too excited. The last time he'd seen Fielding up close was two years ago. They'd been at the same party. Their eyes met across the room, and Fielding had smiled, he'd seen the interest. Fielding wanted to be his and Fielding didn't need to hide it anymore.

They stepped off the elevator, and he followed her down an empty hall.

"Fielding, would you please keep a friend of Little's company until the meeting is over?"

"Of course, I've gotten a little bored waiting for Daddy to finish."

He felt his nose curl up, but made his features relax.

"Be a good boy, and he'll be done soon, then you two can go home. This is Nathan."

"Nice to meet you, Nathan."

He didn't see any recognition in Fielding's eyes, and he clenched his fists in his pockets. He didn't want Fielding to figure out too soon what was happening.

"You, too, Fielding. I might go out for a smoke, so do I need a card key to get out? I saw you swiped one to get into the elevator."

"No, just pick up the phone behind the reception desk and punch in twelve. Fielding can buzz you back upstairs."

"That's great, thank you."

"You two have fun, we should be done in about an hour."

He pivoted on his toes to watch Peaches until she disappeared.

"So, your dad works here?" He glanced back over his shoulder as he asked.

Fielding's cheeks were pink with embarrassment.

"Um, did you want something to drink?"

"That would be great."

He walked across the room, waited for Fielding to turn to the fridge and open it. He pulled out the needle and removed the cap, Fielding straightened, and he struck. He wrapped his arm around Fielding as he plunged the sharp point into the side of Fielding's neck. The dose of the sedative wasn't enough to take the man down, but he couldn't carry him.

Fielding turned to him with wide eyes.

"It took me so long to find you."

145

WHERE WAS HE?

*H*is head pounded as he came to and he looked around the strange cabin. Where was Livingston? He pushed himself to a sitting position and looked around. His head swam, and he started to push himself up, but then it all came back to him. Little's friend. The needle.

He stumbled as he tried to get to his feet as his heart started pounding in his chest. Fear made his dizziness worse, but he had to find a way out.

"Hello, you're finally awake."

A friendly voice caused him to jerk his head around too quickly. Once his vision cleared, he focused on the stranger. The familiar face with deep green eyes and strong features.

"Nigel, what are you doing? I want to go home."

"You are home—well, we'll be going home soon. I'll just give you a day to rest up from your ordeal."

"Livingston's going to find you."

Livingston would find him. He didn't doubt it, and he just needed to hold it together. Be smart. Be strong.

"I seriously doubt that. You don't have to deny what you feel about me. I've known we were meant for each other since the first time I met you. We don't have to hide it anymore."

"You made fun of me with your friends."

"I'm sorry about that, I was stupid, but we don't have to hide it anymore."

"I'm not hiding anything. I want Livingston."

"Your Daddy?"

"He cares about me. He's not—"

He flinched as Nigel's fist connected with the wooden door, and he moved until the bed was between them. The wall held him up because his legs were still weak.

"If I scream people will hear me."

"No, they won't. I found a very nice cabin. Romantic for us to spend the night until we head to my home in the morning. First, we need to take care of a few things."

He'd had a small crush on Nigel until he'd found out how cruel the then sixteen-year-old had been. Condescending and making fun of the other people on set, Nigel thought he was better than everyone else.

"What are you going to do to me?"

"We have to get you clean. You let that disgusting freak touch you. You don't have to pretend anymore; he isn't around. He hurt you, I saw it."

His stomach churned with the need to throw up. "Saw what?"

"You cried after he forced himself on you. He hit you."

Nigel had watched the first night Livingston had taken him. The spanking. He remembered every detail of that night. His first time was special, and he wouldn't cheapen it not even to save himself. Livingston had loved him. "He didn't force himself on me. I loved—"

"Quit lying," Nigel yelled.

The man seemed to calm himself with a few deep breaths and then the friendly smile was back.

"I've got a bath ready for you."

"I don't want a bath. I want to go home to Livingston. Now."

"You need to calm down. We'll have a nice bath, and I'll get you some food, we'll sleep and tomorrow everything will be better."

How crazy was this man? Did Nigel actually think that he wanted anything to do with him?

Nigel moved across the room, and he backed as far into the corner as he could get. He fought the hands that gripped his biceps. He kicked and clawed, but Nigel was surprisingly strong. He was dragged out of the room even as he dug his heels in; the hardwood floors didn't allow him any traction for his sock covered feet.

The sounds of running water and steam filled the bathroom. He was knocked to the floor, and he grunted as his head collided with the old-fashioned tub. The pain dulled his vision. While he was distracted, Nigel snapped cuffs around his wrists and another around his ankles, the metal cutting into his skin.

"Be still I don't want to hurt you."

He shoved himself into the space between the toilet and tub. He stared at Nigel as the man came at him with scissors.

"Stop," he screamed as he tried to kick, but Nigel threw his weight on top of his legs.

He struggled and tried not to choke on his fear as Nigel cut his clothes from him, first his shirt, then his pants and underwear. He curled his body up with fear of Nigel's weight touching his sensitive groin.

"You don't want to do this."

"It's for your own good, Fielding, that brute brainwashed you into thinking you liked those things. I just want to get you clean. I swear I can smell him on you."

He bucked and fought as he was lifted then lowered into the water. Screaming in pain as the scalding water covered him. His skin was turning red. He aimed for Nigel's eyes, but missed, his hands were forced upward, the chain of the cuffs secured over a hook. The bottom of the tub was so slick that he couldn't push himself up far enough to free his hands.

"Now, just relax," Nigel whispered.

It wasn't the thought of getting hurt or whatever Nigel wanted to do to him. No, it was the utter calm in the other man's voice. He could deal with anger. Maybe a hit or two, but Nigel actually believed he wanted that.

He yelled as the rough loofah scraped at his burned skin. Every inch of him was scrubbed. He begged for Nigel to stop when the man reached between his legs.

"You've gotten fat, Fielding, that won't do. We'll get you back into the gym. Muffin tops are not cute."

The man clucked at him, and he slammed his eyes closed as tears filled them. He pictured Livingston. The way Livingston touched him. Loved on him. Relived every time Livingston called him beautiful. He lost himself in the memories as his body was abraded.

Livingston would find him. Livingston promised him.

He could survive this because he knew Livingston wouldn't stop until he brought him home.

HE WAS BRINGING HIS BOY HOME

*H*e watched every second of the videos for a third time since they'd discovered Fielding gone. Rauch had come up behind Fielding. His rage had built the second he saw the needle sink into Fielding's neck. Fielding should have been in the meeting, sitting on his lap, and not alone in the break room. His boy should've been where he belonged.

He pivoted on his toes and grabbed Little's t-shirt. "What the fuck is this shit about a friend of yours visiting you?" He slammed Little back against the wall.

"Dude, I hooked up with someone at Brawlers. Black hair, green eyes, trim, but muscular, that wasn't—"

"Apparently it fucking was and now my fucking boy is gone just because you can't keep it in your pants for anyone who shows you some fucking attention."

If he wasn't so angry, Little's flinch would've made him apologize.

"Livingston, leave Little alone, you can bitch when you haven't fucked up yourself. And I'm just as much to blame. I let the guy upstairs."

Peaches pushed between them, shoving at his chest. And if it were anyone but her, he'd have swung. He jerked away, turning to punch the wall. The pain didn't take the edge off, and he wanted to do it again until his knuckles were bloody.

"This is my office, Livingston, quit abusing it," Hunter chastised him. "Everyone out."

Hunter surged from his chair and pushed everyone out including Linus. Once in the hallway, Livingston calmed down enough to think again.

"Where the fuck would he take him?"

"Cam already set up roadblocks as far out as he could, and Hunter tapped into the camera footage from around town. They headed out of town to the west. He's from Savannah, but he was headed the opposite direction."

He lowered his chin to his chest and drew deep breaths in through his nose and out through his mouth. All he could see behind his lids was Rauch helping a stumbling Fielding out of the break room and into the elevator. That fucker had his boy hidden away somewhere, could be doing—he cut off the thought. Rauch considered Fielding his—thought they had a relationship. The last letters and gifts were the type of thing a boyfriend would give and say. Each letter ended with an I love you.

"There's nothing out that way. There're some lakefront cabins. Old man Hardy hasn't rented those out in a while though. Too much upkeep for him," Linus said.

"Doesn't mean he wouldn't rent them out. Money is money," Little answered.

Luckily Little kept his distance, he still wanted to take the fucker's head off. He shouldn't have said what he did though. Little was on the insane side, but he knew the man's past and Little had some attachment issues. Little always fell hard for someone who showed him some attention. He wanted someone of his own so much Little was a bit gullible when it came to a pretty face.

"I'm on it," Peaches said as she pulled her phone from her pocket.

He held his breath; Fielding was coming up on two hours missing. Their meeting had run over because they'd had to start from square one. He didn't want to think about what Rauch could be doing to Fielding, but the thoughts wouldn't let him go.

"Homer, how are you doing, this is Peaches."

He shoved his hands into his pockets and clenched his fists.

"Well, we've had a friend go missing, and we were wondering if you'd rented out one of your cabins recently...you did, when was that?" Peaches paused. "Two days ago, which one is the young man staying at?"

Peaches rushed to the table and scrawled an address onto one of Gage's legal pads. She picked it up and threw it at him; he caught it.

He was on the move before he hollered for his team to gear up. For all they knew, Rauch was already on the move. He faintly heard Linus talking to Cam to update him. They coordinated that Cam and Wren would meet them at the turn-off.

He had his vest on and was attaching his holster to his thigh.

"Liv."

He ignored Linus.

"Livingston, you have to keep your head in the game. We take Rauch in and hand him over to the Sheriff. This isn't about revenge. You only take that shot if your boy is in danger for no other reason. You got me?"

"Yeah, I got you."

Everyone was in their tactical gear and ready to go when he headed for the elevator. If God turned out to exist, he had enough sins that to pay for one more wouldn't break him.

* * *

HE STARED down the long dirt road that disappeared into the trees. He clenched his fists, and the leather creaked as it stretched over his knuckles. Three hours and time was running out. Rauch seemed to be a highly intelligent man if not completely fucking insane. Would Rauch make the mistake of sticking around after he grabbed Fielding?

"Livingston, you're going in with me and Raul from the east, Little and Pure, you take the west, Gage is going to hang back if we have any problems. Cam and Wren are going in the front to lure Rauch away from the back of the house. We'll make entry, secure the package and be out. No fuck-ups."

Everyone echoed affirmatives behind him.

"Liv, are we good?"

"We're good. I just want Fielding back."

"Only to let him—"

"Shut the fuck up, Linus, I'll do what needs done."

He didn't need Linus or any of the others busting his balls. His boy could already be gone. Delays over bullshit weren't required.

"Let's move," Linus ordered.

He took his usual position of being on point. Wordlessly he let everyone know he'd be the first to enter. He picked through the thick grouping of trees, sidestepped roots and scanning everything in the distance as he kept his gun aimed at the ground.

He stopped just as the cabin came into view and raised his fist to stop Linus and Raul. There wasn't any movement. He glanced toward the road and tracked the slow progress of the Sheriff's SUV. With their distraction in place, they were on the move again.

"We're in position, waiting for orders," Little's voice filled his head from the earpiece.

He crouched down in the shadows as Cam and Wren exited the vehicle.

"On my mark," Linus whispered.

As soon as Cam knocked, he rose from his hiding spot, and as the door opened, Linus gave the order to move in. All the cabins were the same. He stopped on the small stoop and eased open the screen door. He clenched his teeth at the grinding sound. Linus grabbed it, and he tried the handle. It wasn't locked, and he turned the knob and pushed the door open enough for him to squeeze through.

The table was set for a romantic meal, flowers, and candles. Livingston stayed to the edges as he listened to the conversation going on at the front of the cabin.

"Sorry to bother you, sir, but I'm Sheriff Pelter. Mr. Hardy called earlier and said some of his cabins were vandalized overnight. Kids in small towns get bored. We told him we'd check it out."

"It's okay, Sheriff, just doing your job. As you can see everything is fine out here."

"We see that, but law enforcement driving around we didn't want to make you nervous."

He slipped into the hallway toward the single bedroom, and he froze as one of the floorboards creaked under him. He came to a closed door and found a new chain lock. He glanced back to find Linus with his back to him aiming toward the opening of the hall. He raised his right hand and slid the chain free before he opened the door enough to peek in.

As soon as he looked inside, Fielding's sobs became clear.

"Baby," he whispered.

Fielding flew off the bed, and he held his finger to his mouth to tell Fielding to stay quiet. He cursed as Fielding's naked body pressed against his, and he saw the raw, painful looking marks all over him.

"It's okay," he shushed his boy and kissed his soft blond hair. "Do you have some clothes, if not I want you to wrap yourself in a blanket."

"I don't want to—"

"I'll be right here, you're safe, but I need you to cover yourself. Did he—"

"No, no, he scrubbed me, and it hurt, and the water—"

He cut his boy off with a kiss.

"You two can catch up later, let's move." Linus kept his voice low, but his tone was more amused than boss-like.

He flipped Linus off, and Fielding gingerly strode for the bed. Fielding pulled the quilt off the bed.

"Livingston, you take point, and I'll protect your boy's ass."

He nodded as he grabbed Fielding's hand when the boy returned to him and moved him so his boy tucked himself to his back.

"You stay down, and you stay behind me, Raul is waiting in the kitchen, Cam and Wren are at the door."

"Okay." Fielding hugged his waist and pressed his forehead between his shoulder blades.

They were in movement to the end of the hall, and then they heard a shout from the direction of the door. He peeked into the front room to find Rauch face down on the floor fighting Camden's hold.

"Get my boy out," he ordered Linus. "Now, take him."

He felt Fielding fighting Linus, but his boss was stronger, and Fielding was crying behind him. He kept his weapon at his side as he slowly walked across the room and crouched down. He looked into the crazed eyes of Rauch. The fucker didn't even realize he'd been caught.

"My lawyer will have me out in a matter of hours. Can't a man spend the night in a cabin with his boyfriend."

He pressed the barrel of his nine-millimeter to the man's temple.

"Livingston, holster your weapon," Camden ordered.

He had no intention of complying.

"You see, I don't much care about lawyers or even that the Sheriff is putting you in handcuffs. *My* boy is leaving here with me."

"You brainwashed him, he was mine, and you came—"

"Now, now, no need for accusations, Rauch, I can tell you right now, if you even think about coming near Fielding, I don't care if it's a day from now or ten years from now, you're dead. You better be glad I don't want my boy to see me kill you, but I make no guarantees for the future."

He straightened and holstered his weapon; then he spun to find Fielding still fighting Linus' grip. He took a few steps forward and opened his arms. He finally breathed a sigh of relief against Fielding's neck. His arms so tight around his boy with fear that Fielding would disappear.

"We're going to the hospital to get you checked out and then we'll go home, okay?"

Fielding didn't speak simply nodded, and he led his boy out of the house. He only had a little longer with Fielding, and he was going to take advantage of every second.

HIS KNIGHT'S ARMOR WAS PRETTY DENTED

*H*e moaned as Livingston's hands smoothed more of the burn cream over his skin. The tenderness only lasted a few days, but he hadn't told Livingston that. He didn't even know if the man would care that he felt all better.

The first night they were back in the cabin and Livingston had rubbed the medicinal salve into his skin, the big man had been gentle. Even apologized every time he hissed at the pain. He'd had a few blisters from the water. They'd come to find out Nigel had boiled the water on the stove to fill most of the tub.

"My knight in shining armor."

He let his gaze move over Livingston's nude body. He loved the contrast of the hairiness of Livingston's left side and the sparser hair on his right. He felt his mouth pull into a grin as he stroked his palm over Livingston's chest from left to right. He was going to miss this.

Livingston rolled his eyes. "It's pretty dented and rusty if I'm not mistaken."

They hadn't mentioned the future, and in his gut, he knew the big man was going to send him home. It hurt, but he'd do what Livingston said. When Livingston was in Daddy-mode, the man

159

couldn't be swayed. All he could hope for was that Livingston would miss him enough to come for him.

He raised his hand to stroke the big man's scarred cheek. Livingston didn't flinch anymore and seemed to lean into his touch. Probably not to anyone else but him, Livingston gorgeous. Everything he'd ever wanted and was too afraid to find.

"Fielding," Livingston whispered his name and stretched out beside him.

"Don't say it."

"We have to talk about it."

Camden called the day after his rescue to inform them that Nigel had used one of the sheets from a cot to hang himself. Nigel hadn't succeeded in killing himself, but they'd had to transfer him to the psych ward of the local hospital. They assumed he was trying to go for an insanity defense.

"I don't want to…it's over. Nothing happened."

"I've let you get away with not talking about it, but that time has ended."

"He grabbed me, took me to that cabin, tried to boil me in the tub to wash you off me, said I needed to get back to the gym because my muffin top wasn't attractive."

"It's official…he's fucking insane."

He giggled as Livingston bit at the padding in question as the big man's beard tickled him and he combed his fingers through Livingston's dark hair.

"I go home tomorrow."

"I'm sorry."

"Don't be sorry. They say life is about timing, right? Maybe it's just not—"

"That's not what you believe so don't lie to me."

"I want you to keep me. I want to empty out that gaudy apartment my mother decorated for me. I want to live here." Livingston turned his head to rest it on his stomach. "With you. Go to college. I want to be yours, Daddy."

"Being tied to me and all my hang-ups would just make you miserable. I can't do that to you, you're still young, and I was your first."

"Don't say that. I wanted you to be my first. I'll never regret that."

He hated pretending he was feeling mature about this. He wanted to beg Livingston to keep him. The almost two months he'd stayed with Livingston he'd realized that the life he'd had back in California wasn't the one he wanted.

"Fuck me one more time, Daddy, please."

"I don't think—"

"Don't think, please, just one more time and I'll be good when it's time for me to leave."

"I won't fuck you tonight, boy."

He closed his eyes as they started to burn with unshed tears, but then Livingston was on top of him. Livingston's weight was bearing him down into the mattress. He parted his thighs and wrapped his legs around the big man.

Gentle kisses were placed on his face much like the ones when Livingston took him the first time.

"You're so fucking beautiful, and you let me touch you. Did you know you were my first kiss?"

His quickly opened his eyes. "What?"

"The few kisses I'd had, they were drunk, and they still pulled away as soon as they felt my scars. The first time I saw you, I wanted to deny it, but I couldn't look away from you. I wanted your agent or parents to piss off Linus so that he'd tell them to fuck off."

"But you hated me on sight."

"No, little man, I didn't hate you, I wanted you, and I knew you'd find me disgusting and laugh at the freak lusting after someone so out of his league."

"I watched you get ready for bed that night. I didn't care about these." He lovingly stroked the uneven cheek, through his beard to the corner of Livingston's mouth. "I thought you were handsome and dangerous. You know how some of us like those bad boys."

"Is that what it was, nothing about you wanting your Daddy to take care of you?"

"Daddy, if you're not going to fuck me, what are you doing to do with me?"

"I'm going to love on my boy all night."

"Yes, Daddy."

The loving was slow and gentle, the loving Livingston promised him. Kisses and featherlight strokes, Livingston sucking him until he nearly lost it only for the big man to pull back. It was frustrating and perfect. When Livingston's slick fingers readied him, he arched and panted, begged for Livingston to hurry, but the man chuckled and kept up the lazy pace.

He scratched at Livingston's back, tried to tighten his legs to get Livingston with the program. Although, he knew Livingston was in charge—his show.

He gasped at the first nudge of Livingston's cock against his hole, and he arched upward as Livingston filled him. Livingston only paused long enough for him to get used to the pressure. Then he started to move. It was gentle and tender, whispered words of praise and loving touches. They came together in a slow dance, a perfect rhythm, until it wasn't enough.

Livingston pace picked up, but it still wasn't rough. It was a goodbye, and it was bittersweet. Livingston's arms slipped under him, and the big man rested his forehead on his. Livingston hairy stomach stroked his cock with each thrust until he couldn't take anymore. Heat spread between them and Livingston pumped into him faster until Livingston filled him.

"Fuck, I love you so much."

He gasped as he felt hot tears falling on his face as Livingston kissed him repeatedly. He hugged the man's big body to him as the man cried. He knew it was the last thing Livingston was going to say to him.

"It's okay. We're just fine."

"Say it, just one more time."

"I love you, please, keep me."

"I can't. I just want what's best for you, and I'm not it."

He didn't want to argue on their last night together. Livingston always asked him to trust him to know what was best. He'd do that no matter how much it hurt. Livingston started moving inside him again. He wrapped his hands around the sides of Livingston's head and lifted until the man looked at him.

He focused on the scars. All he had to give Livingston was his love, and he'd make sure the man knew it how much he did before he left.

LETTING HIM GO

ielding's parents and agent were scheduled to land any minute. The sun hadn't even started to rise yet, and he stood in the darkness with Fielding against his side. They hadn't spoken since they awakened a few hours ago. He'd taken his boy into the shower and washed him, dressed him between kisses and touches. The morning was for remembering when he was lonely and wanted Fielding beside him.

He understood he was being a bastard, but his fear outweighed his sense. Keeping Fielding would be cruel and not just to Fielding. All his dreams were tucked against his side. All that silly shit he'd made fun of his friends finding over the years turned out to be just what he wanted.

One day Fielding would find someone better who fit into his life. Fielding was it for him. No more drunken hookups. No more out of state trips for just the hope of touch. Last night he'd told Fielding he loved him. He'd wanted to be able to say it once and have it be true. Fielding loved him in return.

He resisted the urge to place a kiss on Fielding's soft hair before he stepped away as the runway lights turned on. He went to retrieve Fielding's bags from the back seat.

Then he returned to Fielding. "Juvie and Princess made a run for me. I put a present in your bag."

"Only a few pieces a day?"

"You're free to do whatever you want."

"Da—"

He couldn't take it. He didn't want to see tears or hear Fielding say those words again.

"Fielding, you said you'd be good."

"And you just told me I'm free to do whatever I want."

Fielding grabbed the front of his jacket and fisted the fabric in his small hands. "I want to stay. I want to wake up with you tomorrow and the day after."

"And you know we can't do that."

"I'm not like everyone else, Livingston. The scars don't matter to me. I love them because—"

Fielding stopped talking as the roar of the plane's engines drowned him out.

"Your parents are going to want to see you."

He swallowed hard around the lump in his throat as Fielding nodded, then turned away from him. He kept distance between him and his boy, forced the mask into place that he'd worn for most of his life. The way he'd wanted Fielding made him forget that this was a job and nothing more. He wouldn't regret that he'd loved Fielding for a short time. It was the happiest he'd ever felt, and he'd always have those memories.

"Fielding." Grant stepped out of the plane and waved.

"You doing okay, man?" Linus leaned to the side to whisper to him.

"I'm fine. I'm taking a week's vacation as soon as he gets on that plane."

"Take as long as you need."

Linus knew he'd take the week to get drunk and he'd want to be alone.

"Mr. Trenton, we want to extend our deepest gratitude for what you and your team did."

"Just doing our job."

"Fielding." Mrs. Haskell's voice made his skin crawl. "You've gained weight. Your cheeks are fat. I told you we didn't have time to get you to lose the weight."

"You're going to ruin your big break, more purge, less binge, Fielding."

He growled at Mr. Haskell and turned to Linus.

"Fuck this shit, boss, may I?"

"Please do." Linus held out his hands for the bags. "I'll put your boy's bags back in the vehicle."

"Boy, come over here," he ordered and watched his boy smile.

"Really?"

"Yes."

Fielding practically ran back to him and launched himself into his arms. His boy wrapped his arms and legs around him.

"I knew you wanted to keep me."

He sunk his fingers into Fielding's hair and jerked his head back.

"May I tell them I'm moving in with you and going to college?"

"Yes, you may."

"Yes," Fielding yelled, and he let the boy slid back to his feet. Fielding danced in a circle before he faced his parents.

His boy was way too excited for something Livingston still didn't know if it was going to work out or not.

"Mother, Father, I'm in love, and I'm staying here with Livingston."

"The hell you are, you're getting on that plane, and leave this silliness behind. You're not gay, and you're not staying here. Even if you were gay, he's completely unacceptable."

"Why, he gorgeous, sweet, bossy, cranky—"

He cut Fielding off by grabbing his hips. "I think that's enough of listing my nicer qualities."

"You're getting on that plane, right now. I'll have you committed, tell everyone the stalker sent you into a nervous breakdown."

"Mrs. Haskell, I suggest you change your tactics." Camden stepped out of the shadows with his arms wrapped around Sin and Saint, Elisabeth strapped to Camden's chest.

"Who the hell are you?"

"I'm Sheriff Camden Pelter; these are my husbands, Eric and Ellison, and our daughter, Elisabeth. Fielding has expressed his wishes to remain with Mr. Livingston. That means you and your party get back on the plane and off my land."

"Shameful, exposing innocent children—"

"Bitch, I don't give a fuck if you're Fielding's mother or not, but you insult my husband again—"

"Eric." Camden's voice held the warning only a Daddy dealing with his boy could pull off.

"Sorry, Daddy, punishment later?"

He covered his mouth to hide his laugh as Sin asked about punishment a little louder than necessary.

"He signed a contract for this movie...he has to come back."

"Then I'll come along and act as security, then bring him home after filming."

"Well, um, I actually don't have a movie to do."

"What are you talking about?" Grant demanded and started to a step forward.

Livingston reached for his weapon, and the man smartened up.

"I called a few days ago, and said that I wouldn't be able to do the movie."

He turned Fielding to face him and raised his hand to place his fingertips under his boy's chin until his boy looked at him. "Fielding, when did you do that?"

"The day Nigel grabbed me, and you were in the meeting. Peaches helped me with all the legal stuff. Peaches was also helping me with getting control of my finances. Even if you weren't going to keep me, I knew I didn't want to live the same way. I thought maybe when I got a bit braver, and I could take care of myself, I'd come back."

"Baby, you don't have to change for me."

"Then why didn't you want to keep me?"

He glanced around, and thankfully Linus and Camden started working crowd control, they ushered bitching parents and a manager back toward the plane.

It was time to be honest. If this was his only chance at his dream, he needed to take it.

"Fear, I didn't want to wake up one day or come home after work one night, and you be sick of me."

Fielding snorted. "You're an idiot."

"Excuse me?"

"I'll take a spanking or whatever for this one. Yes, I'm fifteen years younger than you. I was a virgin before you corrupted me, but that didn't and doesn't make me stupid or immature. My parents wanted a free ride on someone else's dime. I'm pretty so modeling or acting was all I was going to be good for."

He opened his mouth to protest, but his bratty boy arched a brow.

"I did it because I didn't have any other choice...wasn't given one. I told you what I wanted back when you took me for my first ride. That hasn't changed. Your cabin is the first place I've ever felt was home. So, don't make me go back."

"I was just trying to do what I thought was best."

"And I understand that, and I'll trust you to know what's best in every other situation, except this one."

"If I hadn't stopped you, would you have gone?"

"Yes, but not for long. You know, I've become a pretty big Daddy's boy."

Livingston smiled and tipped his head back to stare up at the lightening of the morning sky. He lowered his head back down to study Fielding's delicate features.

"Come on, let's go home. First I'll punish for being bratty, and after that, I may reward you if you're a good boy and take your punishment."

"Yes, Daddy."

"Brat." He grabbed Fielding's hand and led him back to the vehicle. He opened the door, helped his boy inside and buckled him in so he was safe.

"Livingston," Linus yelled his name. "You still taking that weeks' vacation?"

"Don't even think of calling me."

He got into the driver's seat listening to his best friend laugh his fucking head off.

"What's so funny?" Fielding asked.

"My friends are idiots."

"I kinda like your friends. We going camping again?"

The question was asked too sweetly, and he snarled at a smirking Fielding.

"No, not anytime soon."

"They're sweet. They may need some company. All lonely in the woods by themselves."

"That right there means you're never going camping again."

He started the SUV and backed up until he could turn around and head for home. He hoped Fielding knew what he wanted because once he got him home, it was too late for his boy to change his mind.

OF COURSE HE WAS GOING TO SAY YES

*H*e shivered as he threw more logs on the fire and was thankful Livingston wasn't home from work yet. His Daddy loved to make fun of him for being cold all the damn time. He'd been there four months and still wasn't used to the cold. A knock rattled the door, and he ran to look out the window. Little was standing on the porch.

Oh shit, what the hell was he doing here? He slowly walked to the door debating whether to answer it or not.

Livingston didn't like anyone other than them in the house, but then a thought hit him. He threw open the door. "Is Livingston okay?"

"Oh fuck, yeah, damn, I didn't think, sorry, I wanted to talk to you for a minute."

"Sure, let me get my coat."

"Daddy not here so you can ask his permission?"

"I'm being respectful of his wishes, and he's on a takedown so I can't call him." He lifted Livingston's leather jacket from the hook beside the door and stepped outside as he was slipping it on.

"Sorry, I sounded like an ass."

"It's okay. What did you want to talk about?"

J.M. DABNEY

Little hung his head and stared at the toes of his scuffed boots. "I wanted to apologize for putting you in danger."

"Little, you didn't know, and we learned he was good at disguises."

"They told me my mom dropped me off at social services when I was five. Told them I was crazy and she couldn't take it anymore. Don't know who my dad was or even if he knew he had a kid. I read all my reports once. Basically, they said I was excessively clingy. Had some attachment disorder and separation anxiety. Said I became unnaturally attached when I was shown affection."

"Little, you don't have to explain."

The misery on the man's face broke his heart. Little was odd that couldn't be denied, but everyone he'd met since coming to Powers was a bit on the weird side. It was their charm. He didn't want the man to feel bad about the way he was—Little's life made him have his issues.

"I do, Livingston said I put you in danger because I couldn't see past a pretty face showing me affection. He was right. I fucked Rauch because it's the only way people let me touch them. I know I'm scary looking and I'm not all there, but I ain't all bad."

"Little, you don't have to apologize because you wanted some human contact. I believe you didn't know who Rauch was."

"Livingston's still mad at me. I thought if I apologized and explained that maybe one of my best friends wouldn't be mad at me anymore. The people I've met here are the only family I got. I can't lose them."

"And you won't, I'll talk to Livingston when he gets home."

"Liv is lucky to have you. It must be nice."

"What must be nice?"

"To be touched."

The man's deep voice broke over the last word, and he almost reached out to stroke Little's huge bicep, but the man stepped back.

"Little, do you—"

"No, I overstayed, I'm on cheating spouse duty tonight."

172

Little practically ran from the porch and to the black van. They joked that Little lived in it. Little didn't look back at him, and he quickly backed out, headed down the dirt road.

His phone beeped in his pocket, and he pulled it out. Livingston sent him a message telling him he was on his way home. He removed his jacket and hung it back up as he went to find something to make for dinner. They needed to do a supply run soon. They couldn't live on love and sex alone. He was going to lose his belly that Livingston loved so much.

An hour later, he was just taking the chicken and rice casserole he'd thrown together with stuff he'd found in the freezer out of the oven. He placed it on the stovetop. The door opened, and he glanced up to find Livingston still in his tactical gear. He ran across the room, and Livingston caught him with a grunt.

"You grunted, am I getting too—"

"You even say that word, or I'll put you over my knee before this nights over with."

"Don't you do that anyway?"

"You're getting awfully bratty, baby."

He pouted, and Livingston smiled.

"I was headed home to take you out to dinner and then grocery shopping afterward."

"I found enough stuff to make a casserole. Plan for it tomorrow?"

"Sure, what did you do today?"

"Well, I applied for the fall semester of college, I'll need to get a vehicle to commute."

He draped his arms over Livingston's strong shoulders and batted his lashes at him.

"You have to learn to drive first."

"That's where my gorgeous Daddy comes into play."

"We'll go get your learner's and then look at a nice safe car for you next week. I may also need to take up drinking."

"It won't be that bad. Little stopped by."

"And why was Little here."

Livingston walked toward the kitchen and sat him on the counter, then Livingston gave him a quick kiss and pulled away.

"Don't get pissed, he wanted to apologize, and he said you're still mad at him. He doesn't want to lose the only family he has."

"I'm not mad, I get Little and his quirks. The man just frustrates the fuck out of me. We need to find him a person to latch on to."

"I don't think he needs a person to latch on to as you so sweetly put it. He just needs someone who's going to love him."

"Little makes it hard to love him and the person who does is going to have to be a full-time keeper. He's spent way too much time with Lily. I think she's made him worse."

"He's fine. I just wanted you to know and quit making him feel bad. He just wanted to feel needed even if it was just sex."

"Fine, I'll talk to him tomorrow. Now, since you ruined my plans to take you out all romantic like, you'll have to settle for this."

"What are you talking about? Aren't you going to change and get comfortable before we have dinner?"

"I know how hard it is for you to say no when I'm in my work gear, so I wanted to ask you something." Livingston pushed his thighs wide and stepped his big body between them.

"And what did you want to ask me, Daddy?"

He started to grin until Livingston reached into a tiny pocket on his vest and pulled out a thin black band. He quickly glanced up at Livingston to find the man studying him, but he couldn't read Livingston's expression.

"I never really thought about the whole marriage thing, and I know people don't need the whole piece of paper and all that to prove anything. I just want everyone to know you're mine."

"Like something you can show off, like look I got something pretty on my arm? I require vows. Party. The whole thing. You're going to make an honest man out of me."

"Fielding."

"Ew, you used my name, put it on so you can spank me."

"What?"

"Put the damn ring on, now." He held out his hand. "Right here." He wiggled his finger.

"I don't think you deserve it."

"What will make me deserve it?"

"Undress."

He'd never get tired of his man's gruff voice—dangerous and commanding. Two months ago, Livingston told him he wasn't going home, but he still couldn't get his head around how lucky he felt to belong to Livingston. His Daddy took care of him. Always made sure he was happy and safe. He never went without anything.

"Yes, Daddy."

He bit his lips to hide his smile as Livingston lifted him off the counter, then the man stepped away from him to pull out one of the kitchen chairs. He slowly removed his clothes as he watched Livingston remove his holster and laid it carefully on the table.

He pushed his sleep pants off his hips and let them fall, kicking them aside when they pooled around his ankles.

His face flushed as he stepped forward and Livingston patted his lap. He shivered as he rested his stomach on Livingston's hard thighs. Livingston's forearm came to rest on his lower back. The rough pads of Livingston's fingers and palm scraped seductively over the curves of his ass that was fuller than it was when he'd moved there. He didn't have to starve or torture himself anymore, he still worked out, but he didn't need to kill himself in the process.

"I think you've earned twenty, if you lose count I start again, boy, do we understand each other?"

"Yes, Daddy."

He braced himself for the first strike, when it came he flinched and counted. The more he was punished, the harder it became to keep counting. His cock hardened against Livingston's thigh. Livingston gentled him between smacks, soothing the burn to intensify it with the next time his hand connected with his burning, abused flesh.

He barely remembered to say twenty before he collapsed over Livingston's lap. He was lifted off Livingston's lap before being pulled down and cuddled. Livingston kissed the tears from his cheeks. Traced his wet lashes with the tip of his tongue.

"Can I have it now, Daddy, please?"

"Give me your hand."

He raised his left and Livingston slipped the cool metal onto his ring finger.

"So, is this a yes?"

"Of course I was going to say yes. You said you didn't think you could be happy without me. I don't think, no, I know I couldn't be happy without you. I love you."

"I love you too. Thank you."

He pressed a soft kiss to Livingston's small smile.

EPILOGUE

KILLING LITTLE WOULD BE THE HIGHLIGHT OF HIS WEDDING DAY

*H*e glared at Little who was shielded by Sin, Saint, Fielding, and Lily. The supposed hippie looked pissed enough to commit murder because he'd threatened her precious adopted pain in the ass son. Linus, Pure, and Raul were holding him back as he clenched his jaw.

"Don't make me arrest every fucking last one of you today," Camden roared from his spot on the porch. He already had his service weapon out and pointed at them.

"What the fuck did I do? Your boys, my boy, and Little along with Little's bestie, Lily, decided a party south of the border sounded like a good idea. I think I have a right to kill his fucking ass. It will be the highlight of my wedding day. If your father-in-law hadn't been around to fly Peaches down, my boy would still be in jail."

Sin and Fielding were trying to hold in their giggling. He didn't know how much they smoked on the way home, at least Saint had behaved himself enough to fly.

"I'll handle my own boys, and who the fuck woke up in one of my jail cells this morning?"

"I didn't throw that first fucking punch. That fucker was asking for it."

He'd been minding his own business when the stripper Little sent to Brawlers tried to get in his lap, and the man's boyfriend showed up. The asshole boyfriend got a little rough with the stripper, and he'd knocked the fucker out. He was doing a public service.

"Livingston, do you want to get married in jail today?"

"No," he pushed out through gritted teeth.

"Now, get in the fucking house and get your suit on, and, no fucking in my house. Eric, Ellison, in the house now."

"Yes, Daddy," Sin and Saint said in unison and slowly ascended the steps.

Camden swatted both of them as they passed and he shook his head at the big man.

Camden let out a heavy sigh. "I'm too old for this shit."

"Fielding, let's go get ready, and, Little, we'll finish this later."

"You put your hands on my son, Livingston, and I'll make your boy a widower." Lily wrapped her arms around Little's waist and led him away toward his van.

"I think Lily would do it," he whispered to Fielding as he nudged his boy toward the house. "What the hell were you thinking?"

"They said they were taking me somewhere. I thought Vegas or something like that, I didn't know we were going to Mexico, and Lily had friends there. It wasn't like I could fly myself back."

"You want to run off to Vegas and skip this whole freak show?"

"Lily would kill you a second time if you don't let her perform the wedding."

"We can run away and never be seen from again."

"I'm sorry, I really didn't think—"

"It's fine. I shouldn't have gotten mad. I know these people too well." He led him into a small downstairs bedroom and closed the door. "Do you still want to marry me?"

"Um, are we going to have this talk today? If you didn't want to marry me all you had to do—"

He slammed his mouth down on Fielding's to shut him up.

"I didn't say that; our lives aren't going to be normal. Have you seen our friends?"

"Those aren't friends, Daddy, that's family."

"I preferred being an orphan."

"Get all handsome for me. I've been dying to see you in your tux."

"I do love you, Fielding."

"I love you too. I'm going to wash off the stench of weed and jail. I'll be right back. Don't leave."

"I'll never leave you."

Fielding lifted onto his toes to kiss him again and went into the bathroom. There was a knock on the door, and he opened it to find Peaches standing there. She looked beautiful in a cream-colored linen dress that made her tattoos and the thread wraps in her hair appear brighter.

"Hey."

"Can I come in and talk to you for a minute?"

"Sure, you look beautiful by the way."

"Thanks, Gib had Lucky make it for me."

"What's going on?"

She took his hands and held them in hers. "Lily already did the whole groom's mother thing with Fielding, but I threatened her to stay away from you."

"You don't have to do anything special, Peaches."

"Yes, I do. When you started attending our crazy little family things I began watching you. You always stood to the side, out of the way where no one could see you, but I did, Livingston, I saw you. I saw the sadness in your eyes. That longing no one else would notice. When I saw Fielding, I knew he would be perfect for you, but I also understood why you'd send him home."

"I didn't think I was best for him."

"You're just as deserving of love as the rest of us. He looks at you like you're the only man in the room. You did good, son, you met your person, and he is so lucky to have you. Almost as lucky as I am to have you for a son."

She released his hands and brought them to his cheeks, and then she tugged him down to place soft kisses on his left cheek then his scarred one. Lingering a few seconds longer and he closed his eyes.

"Congratulations, son, this is for you to give your young man."

She reached into a pocket on her dress and pulled out a black box. She flipped it open to expose a locket with an intricate design of a skull with crossed roses instead of bones.

"You always joked about being the beast without the escape clause, but you didn't need to be anything but yourself."

She turned back toward the door, opened it and stepped back out. He glanced at the bathroom as he heard the click of the lock. He awkwardly worked the tiny closure on the locket and found a picture of him and Fielding at their engagement party. Fielding looked so happy, but the surprising thing was he looked even more so as he looked down at his boy. He'd finally learned to live, and all it took was a bratty boy and a dysfunctional extended family.

He sensed Fielding watching him.

"Thank you for loving me."

"For that, Livingston, you never have to thank me."

THE END

ABOUT THE AUTHOR

J.M. Dabney is a multi-genre author who writes mainly LGBT romance and fiction. She lives with a constant diverse cast of characters in her head. No matter their size, shape, race, etc. she lives for one purpose alone, and that's to make sure she does them justice and give them the happily ever after they deserve. J.M. is dysfunction at its finest and she makes sure her characters are a beautiful kaleidoscope of crazy. There is nothing more she wants from telling her stories than to show that no matter the package the characters come in or the damage their pasts have done, that love is love. That normal is never normal and sometimes the so-called broken can still be amazing.

www.ingramcontent.com/pod-product-compliance
Lightning Source LLC
Chambersburg PA
CBHW060156130626
46556CB00006B/2661